War of Kings

Wind of Destiny, Volume Six

AJ Cooper

SANCTON
THE BLESSED ISLES
Eloesus
RIVER SULIS
PALLISTRIX
ISTEROS
ARCTOS
100 mi.
200 mi.
300 mi.
400 mi.
500 mi.
AGATHÉ
TIGRIS
IOGHEIRA
STRAITEIRA
THÉNAI
THENOA
KERSEPOLI
KERSICA
KORTHOS
KORTHICA
TEN CITIES
THARTA
THARTICA
ARKADIOS
THEMURIA

THE INDWELLING

Rogon's arm was lifted; he did not raise it.

Or so he thought.

As he lay there in the burning sun, his movements were part his and part alien.

He had died. He had left this world. He had entered the land of the shades, consumed with cold fire. In agony he had cried out in the River of Souls; and then, in the blink of an eye, he was back in Varda, back in the sun's warmth, back on the green earth.

Yet as he rose, he did not feel entirely himself. There was something strange, something alien, something horrific taking hold.

He rose with a new strength.

THE TINKERER

Agathion had spent hours locked in the tower, fitting—with a spyglass—gears and wires which could scarcely be seen by the naked eye.

At last, his ten years of work were finished: ten years, every day, from dusk till dawn, before he finished his first automaton.

One by one he began screwing in the brass plates, until they formed a human-like body, mounted on a ball. He screwed on the iron framing; he fixed the jewels to the eye socket. Then, opening his cask of lightning, he unleashed the energy needed.

The once lifeless figure of bronze stirred to life. The ball on which it was mounted began to roll this way and that, and then around the room.

Its bronze hand, which held a sword, began to swing with dizzying speed.

"Hush!" Agathion cried, and clapped his hands.

The automaton slumped downward and stopped its movement.

Agathion began to leap up into the air. "I have done it!" he cried. "I have done it!"

HIGH CITY, THÉNAI

From this perch on Thénai's High City, where Theron could survey the world, he took a good look of what was offered him, and balked.

He could control the Thenoan League; a virtual kingship was offered to him.

But his destiny lay beyond. Far out there was Mount Hylea, the holy place where the Oracle still ruled. The Oracle and her maids sought to kill him. They had betrayed his trust. They had betrayed their allegiance to Eloesus. His enemies were many, and they wanted him dead; but of all enemies the Oracle was the most cunning and deviant. Once he—like all Eloesians—thought the Oracle was a force for good, but now he knew it wasn't true. There was darkness in the Oracle's heart, a darkness deeper than that of any killer.

Khloë stood beside him, sabers in hand.

"Will you go with me?" Theron asked. "To the Mount of Prophecy?"

"I will follow you to the ends of the earth," Khloë answered.

~

By dusk, they had exited Lion's Gate and begun their long journey, up and down a winding road. The sun set behind them, sinking beneath the western hills.

THE GOLD GARTER, THÉNAI

A fire burned bright and furiously in the hearth. Over Gaia's gold robes she had covered herself in a shawl. Yet there was a chill she could not stave off, the chill of fear, the chill of dread.

She had in her hand a flagon of Khazidean beer, which—in all its deliciousness—she had not tried before. Yet the strong mixture did not do enough to help her forget.

She had placed the Gauntlet of the Demiurge on Rogon's hand—and he had stirred to life. Once dead, he now lurked just outside the city walls.

~

Though she had drunk six flagons and eaten a hearty meal of bread and lamb, Gaia nevertheless entered her sleeping quarters nervously, without any semblance of calm. Her ship back home didn't leave for three days; and she didn't want to spend any more time here, in this foreign place, than she had to.

Her servants, sleeping in a spare room, had a decidedly worse situation. And yet they were not scarred by the images of the demiurge's Gauntlet; they did not witness the body of Rogon, stirred to life again by some unseen spirit. They had not been haunted for months; violated in their privacy by the appearance of the demiurge.

A light rain began to fall, pattering on the rooftop. She opened the shutters of the window and saw the water drip down. Lightning struck in the distance; moments later, thunder rolled.

The wind blowing through the open shutters began to turn cold. She shut them, and closed the latch. She locked her door and made sure it wouldn't budge. She undressed. Despite the flagons of Khazidean beer, she felt unwell. Her stomach was twisted to knots. She was afraid to go to sleep.

Despite her mother's frequent warnings when Gaia was a child, she did not blow out her candle. She could not bear the darkness. She knew the evil things which lay in its shadow. In the light of the candle, she still struggled to sleep, looking above at the cheap, caving-in ceiling covered in the dirt and dust of hundreds of lodgers. The room had the scent of mold and mildew. Twice she saw a roach scuttle along the bare-bones wooden floor.

And this was the best inn she could find in the harbor!

Yet with time, with an hour, exhaustion proved stronger than fear. She closed her eyes and drifted off into a deep, deep sleep.

~

She awoke in the manner that she feared most, paralyzed and unable to move, breathless and ice cold. Her breath turned to fog. The light of the candle was no comfort as the shadowy form of the demiurge stepped out from her closet.

Like a man in armor, but all in shadow, the only jarring thing in his black, featureless, silhouette were two red eyes. He approached her and all the roaches under her bed scuttled away, out of the room and under the door. His breath was like ice. The demiurge bent over her, stretching his body until she could no longer avoid his glaring red eyes. Burning like beacons in a black canvas, they examined her, saw her, viewed her deepest vulnerabilities, her fears, her flaws. The demiurge fed on her fear, on her weakness, on her utter helplessness. He delighted in her terror.

"Why?" she cried—the demiurge had released the paralysis in her mouth—"Why? You said you would leave me alone… after

I gave you your Gauntlet. You said you would go away…"

She was weeping.

The demiurge stretched out his body. His eyes burned brighter. If there were any detail to his face, perhaps there would be a great gaping grin. "And yet I am not done with you Gaia… you still have a role to play."

Back into the shadows the demiurge slipped, slinking until he had vanished into the darkness of the closet.

Gaia cursed her fate.

~

For what ailed Gaia, there was no drug, no potion or poison that an apothecary could mix.

She was weary the next morning, unable to function. Though the innkeeper had cooked fat pork sausages and poured Gaia a great goblet of wine, everything seemed to lack taste, and the world had lost some of its color.

"Can I help you, my lad—"

"Hush!" Gaia snapped at her servant. Once she'd eaten a pork sausage and grown sick of food altogether, she took out a mirror to brush her hair and apply cosmetics.

The face she saw was one she did not recognize.

That face was pale, and bags were under its eyes; the exhaustion from months and months of torment by the demiurge had taken a toll on her.

Still, she brushed her hair, and dabbed her eyelashes with Ink-of-Tyrhenos. Her Powder-of-Adamantis was not required; her face was pallid and white already. She colored her lips with red ointment, ran a comb through her hair, and realized—after all she'd been through—this was the best she could do.

One of her servants, a southron woman, came up to dote

on her.

"Your Worship," she said, with her antiquated, autocratic lexicon. "I've prepared a bath for you."

"I didn't ask for one," growled Gaia. She had no time for this. She had no time for any of this.

She dropped her mirror on the table. Patrons of the inn were gawking at her like she was a crazy woman.

And perhaps she was. This phantasm was all she thought about; how to fight it, how to stop it, how to shake the demiurge's grip on her life.

~

Out in the bustling streets of Thénai, signs of the city's prosperity were all around. The streets were paved white with fine stones; at every street corner, it seemed, there was a bronze statue—of crossroads gods and guardian spirits. Along the streets, the noise was overwhelming and omnipresent; the rattling of chariots and the shouting of street vendors was a perpetual sign of commerce.

Korthos had the greatest military minds and the greatest fighting force; but could they compete against such life and liberty?

Gaia had a headache. She had not slept well.

The city air, with its smoke and scent of waste, did little to soothe her.

And she needed no soothing. She needed curing… curing from the curse of the demiurge, and the long shadow he cast over the world. She had to escape his grip, through any means necessary.

Where could she go? Where could she find a cure from haunting?

A temple was her best option. She turned her eyes to Thénai's High City, and wondered if the marble-pillared wonder—soaring above the city—would be her salvation.

From far away, the scent of incense was thick. There were voices singing and cymbals clashing.

The Temple of Tyros—once the Temple of Amara—was so tall and towering in scope that it seemed the heavens rested on its roof. Friezes in bright blues, yellows, and reds told a story of amazons and humans fighting. At the steps the priest had gathered with some common worshippers; they were singing and leaping up and down.

The priest of Tyros had a long silver beard. He was painted blue according to some ritual; the frenzied worshipers were clearly under the influence of some potion or drug. As they struck the cymbal and sang songs about Tyros' bravery in battle, Gaia passed them by. She walked up the steps and entered.

A statue stretched to the roof of the temple: from the neck down a man, from the head up a bear.

This was the idea of Tyros which Isteroi barbarians had.

In truth, it was a sacrilege to have this image here, this half-beast which degraded the holy gods.

"Woman." A priest was walking toward her.

Perhaps he noticed her scowl, her disgust at the barbarian display here.

"You are on sacred ground." There was an edge to the priest's voice.

There was a ritual to undergo before entering a temple.

Gaia had not set foot in a sacred space in years. A cleansing bath, a removal of shoes—she felt like a rustic from the countryside, now. But she wouldn't apologize. She met the priest's gaze directly. She said, "I need help."

The priest sported a long gray beard. His clothing was sewn to resemble armor. In his right hand was a club—ceremonial, but carved to look like a weapon. His robes were dyed blue and white. "Help," he repeated. "Do you think Tyros cares for the weak, dying on the battlefield? When he turns the tide of war to an army, do you think he considers the sick and the wounded?"

Gaia sneered. She'd never put much stock in religion. She still didn't. If there was a god or a life force which permeated existence, it wasn't a human conception. It certainly wasn't a man with a bear's head.

"You don't believe, do you," said the priest. "How can I help you if you don't believe?"

~

In the privacy of an inner room, with the door closed, Gaia told the priest what ailed her.

The story of the Gammahedron and the demiurge's shadowy hand elicited a gasp from the otherwise stoic priest.

As she regaled her nightmares and moments of panic, she caught the priest inching away from her, as if he didn't want to catch her disease.

When at last she finished, and she spoke of the Gauntlet, the priest stood up angrily.

"You did the bidding of a demon," the priest snarled, "and you ask for my help."

Gaia looked up at him. Her eyes welled with tears. Would he attack her now, now that she had exposed everything, that she had uttered her deepest, darkest secrets? "I did not know," she said.

"You ventured into Mount Kronos! Mount Kronos! Named after the Lord of Chaos himself... surely that would enlighten you on the matter!"

What could Gaia have expected from a priest? Understanding? Mercy? Of course not. All her beliefs on priests and religion were reaffirmed in this moment. "Goodbye," she said, and left the temple, weeping.

HILL COUNTRY, THENOA

They were a day outside Thénai, setting up camp. They had a little food and a little water, but not enough to last the whole journey. Khloë would have to hunt.

The stars were bright and clear—brilliant and luminous in the absence of the city's smoke and lanterns.

Khloë poked the logs as she tried to get the fire going.

Her mind was caught up in the whirl of events that had transpired.

She had begun to doubt the path she was taking.

They had left the city leaderless.

As the fire caught on, the flickering light illuminated Theron, still wearing a lion skin. He was swarthy, dark, handsome. Every woman in Thénai wanted him; but there were higher concerns on his mind, concerns which affected the whole nation. Love and lust were petty matters, compared to that.

And yet, over these months, Khloë had nursed an attraction to him, an attraction which she had kept secret, which she did not want to mention. She was afraid of what he might do, afraid of what he might say, if she confessed it to him.

As the night set in and a cold wind blew, Khloë stood up. "I have to go back," she said.

"Go back," Theron repeated. He looked angry. "To Thénai?"

"Their king is dead. They have no leader," Khloë said. "All those thousands of people… we can't just toss them aside, Theron. We can't just throw them out."

Judging by Theron's glare, he thought they could.

But there were greater things at stake than just him. The stability of the region, the check which Thénai provided against the aggressive, violent Kersican League—all that had to be considered.

Theron stood up, grabbing his club. "You aren't going."

You aren't going – Khloë repeated the words in her head. Theron should have said what he meant—"you aren't going to leave me alone." There was fear in his voice. He did not want to face the Oracle or her Maids of Prophecy without Khloë. He did not believe he could overcome them without her help.

But Theron didn't know his own strength, or the power of his convictions. No one on earth could deter Theron when he was determined. He could shake the earth's foundations.

And yet Khloë hesitated, unsure for a moment, as the fire caught on in full, casting away the darkness of the night. Could she abandon him here and now? Could she disobey him? His dark eyes, sullen and angry, almost broke her away. "I'm leaving," she said. "Thénai needs me."

HILL COUNTRY, THENOA

Theron watched Khloë's form disappear into the darkness.

She did not understand the way her abandonment made him felt. She did not understand the depth of her betrayal.

Forces were at work, forces more powerful than Kronos ever was. Those forces wanted Theron dead.

He had thought Khloë was loyal to him. He had thought Khloë cared about him.

No more. He was alone. All his problems, he would have to solve himself. All the dangers, he would have to face alone.

He listened to the cicadas sing. Against that background, and the crackle of the fire, he tried to listen to footsteps, to breaking twigs, to anything indicating he could be followed.

Without Khloë there wasn't a second pair of eyes or another listening ear; he was infinitely more vulnerable. Khloë knew that, surely. She was aware of it; and chose Thénai—the city that had betrayed him.

He wrapped his club with a cloth and drizzled it with oil. He set it alight until it became a flaming brand. The fine wood, or whatever *Titan's Fist* was carved from, refused to burn.

He headed into the woods, seeing nothing in the shadows of the trees, but the darkness was deep and extended far beyond the makeshift torch's reach.

The oaks and cypress trees were bright and green in the light of day; but here, illuminated only by the feeble brand, the darkness beyond them was menacing.

Despite himself, Theron was panicking. *I have no reason to fear,* he told himself.

Then, at the edge of his vision, he caught sight of a Maid of Prophecy scurrying away.

Am I hallucinating? Am I losing my mind?

His mind… what was left of it?

He turned and saw, at the edge of the darkness, the form of a Maid of Prophecy—again—slipping into the darkness.

He was surrounded.

The flaming brand would soon run out of fuel.

Ahead was a Maid of Prophecy. She was carrying an olive branch.

Theron charged her; within moments, he had caught up to her. He set upon her. He raised his club.

He pushed her to the ground. He could not hurt this woman. "What do you want from me? Why are you trying to kill me?"

He turned again. The flames illuminated two more Maids of Prophecy. Both held olive branches in their hands.

"Lay down your arms!" a woman cried.

He turned in the direction of her voice, and saw a woman clothed in white linen, bearing a sword.

The flaming brand was burning bright, for now, but it would fade. He was encircled by the Maids of Prophecy; he could see their faces, dozens of them, positioned around him, olive branches in hand.

"There are forces at work," said the woman with the sword. "Forces which you do not understand."

The rage building up these past weeks was rising up within him. "Who do you think you are?" he shouted at her.

"Lay down you arms!" she commanded him again.

The gall!

He would slay every one of these Maids of Prophecy. Then he would ascend the Mount of Prophecy and bludgeon the Oracle to death.

He charged the woman with the sword, and unflinchingly swung back his club, intending to crush her skull; she stepped inward, tripping him, and sent his club flying. In an instant the Maids of Prophecy were upon him, binding his arms and legs with rope. He cursed and struggled; the rope showed signs of tearing. Then a cloth was forced upon his mouth, and he fell asleep.

THE GOLD GARTER, THENAI

Gaia had one more day before the ship left its port, before—gods forbid a storm—she would arrive at home, alone, powerless in Korthian government, with a husband who wouldn't speak to her, but safe.

She would be secure, save the nightmares that were draining her life away. She would still face the machinations and oppressions of the demiurge; but she would do so in her home, in her own city, and not behind enemy lines.

Once she'd finished her breakfast of berries and cream, Gaia asked for instructions to the apothecary. If priests refused to help her, and if the gods would not relent in the curse, then medicine was all she had left.

~

Down Thénai's packed-full, bustling streets, through the carriages running wild and the merchants shouting from makeshift stalls, around several corners and down several dim-lit streets, Theto's Potions and Elixirs could be found. It faced a narrow street, where the roof blocked out the oppressive sun. Its front was faced with glass.

On shelves, along the glass, there were pots where flowers and plants grew—white tulips, bright red roses, thorny vines, even a deadly flytrap. This Theto was a man who knew his trade. If anyone could help Gaia, Theo the Apothecary could.

She entered through the door and was hit with a wave of scents, all of them potent and pungent, setting her sinuses on fire. Beyond the store window, shelves and shelves of jars were on display.

When Theto emerged from the jungle of shelves and pots, Gaia was surprised at the sight of him—skinny and seemingly malnourished. He was lanky, and the gloves on his hands were stained with red soil. "Greetings," he said.

"What can I help you with?" Theto said. A grin grew on his face. "I see by your clothing you are a lady of some distinction… but I have very rich clientele. You want night's eye."

Gaia scoffed. The plant which grew in the rivers of Khazidea, was dried and crushed to a powder and mortars and pestles, caused psychotic hallucinations. Sorcerers used them to achieve a higher state of mind; in back alleys and in private chambers it was consumed recreationally.

"Never," Gaia answered. The night's eye weed had never entered her body, nor would it.

"What plagues you?" Theto asked.

What was he expecting her to say, she wondered. Perhaps, he thought Gaia was just another rich woman suffering from the gout. How many wealthy clients had come in here, suffering from diseases of affluence, obesity, redfoot, or the ache.

It was clear people of Gaia's stature came here quietly to procure night's eye.

Was a plague of nightmares the ultimate "rich man's disease?"

Perhaps Gaia should feel lucky that the very thing that was killing her was something everyone experienced, and no one complained about.

She was hesitant, now, to tell Theto what bothered her. Yet anyone looking at her could see something was wrong; she was pallid and she had lost weight over these months. She slept only an hour or two a night. In the daytime she was dazed and deprived of energy. Several times a day she broke into weeping at her misery, as the demiurge continued to cast his long shadow over her.

"Nightmares," she answered Theto, "nightmares like you wouldn't believe. Nightmares that are killing me."

"Nightmares won't kill you," Theto said.

"Ha!" Gaia cursed at him. "You have no idea. I am dying…" Even those who doubted the deadliness of nightmares could see she was deteriorating. "I am cursed… by a demon… the demiurge…"

Theto's eyes widened. This is a crazy woman, he likely thought.

But Gaia wasn't crazy. In her youth, she'd had nightmares after hearing a scary story or witnessing a death; but this was something altogether different. The demiurge was real, even if no one believed her.

"Nightmares," said Theto. "I'll try to find something for you."

There were jars of named ingredients, such as mercury or lead; there were jars only labeled with "for fever" or "for aches." It seemed Theto knew them all by heart.

"For fear." He stopped in front of an unmarked jar.

When he portioned out the medicine, Gaia recognized its color and scent. This was night's eye.

Night's eye was illegal in Korthos. Its manufacture and distribution was totally forbidden. But if this would stop the nightmares, as Theto seemed to think, Gaia would do anything.

"Are you sure?" Gaia asked. Her voice trembled.

"Night's eye," Theto said with a grin, "yes, I am sure."

He was an addict. His thinness and emaciation made it clear. That meant his bias was evident as well.

Gaia, at the edge of collapse, would try anything. Even this.

That night, the night before she boarded her ship, the demiurge did not visit her.

Instead, she saw the world shake; the walls, of Thénai, tremble, and in the distance, the form of her lover Rogon, rising from the grave.

The ship was leaving Thénai, bearing cargoes of olive oil and perfume. The ship would arrive in Korthos in a manner of days, provided there was no storm. With Gaia and her servants there were others, intending to take a second ship to Dys.

Gaia had not taken her medicine yet. But she felt at ease.

THE LION'S GATE, THÉNAI

When Khloë at last saw the City of Thénai in all its walled splendor, she cast aside her walking stick and hurried into its embrace.

So many still despised her as an amazon; but many attempted to be welcoming. In Thénai, unlike Korthos, she had the full rights of citizenship under the law.

Its streets were familiar. Though the air was smoky and poor in quality, though the ways and avenues were crowded with people, she felt like she had arrived at home.

And yet, as she ascended to the heights of the High City, there were signs she was not welcome. Some, passing up and down, uttered words to their neighbor or glared at Khloë outright. She was not one of them. She would never be one of them. She was a Thenoan citizen, according to temple records; but she was an amazon. She did not belong here.

At the Temple of Tyros she paused. She looked down at the city—its buildings tiny at this great height, its smoke wafting up into the heavens, its ships buzzing through the harbor—and wondered if she should leave. Amazonia would accept her. She was an amazon; she would always be an amazon. Ships were heading westward; would Tigris or Kolkis be a port of call? Would those vessels take their cargoes to the Amazonian heartland of Jogheira, or to the hinterlands of Far Kalormenë?

In the end she turned toward the colonnades of the House of the Archon. For now, at least, she would stay.

The halls of the House of the Archon retained their marble gleam, their gold-bordered paintings, their statues and their works of art. A group of servants were scrubbing the floors; another, in the distance, polished a silver bowl. Everything was subdued. The city was leaderless… in crisis. If war broke out, Thénai and all the allies it was supposed to protect would be in serious danger.

"The archon," Khloë said to the group of servants. "Where is he?"

A young maid answered. "He is with Bat Zor."

Back down the ramp, descending from the heights of the High City, she entered once again the world of the land-dwellers.

City Square's beautification project was almost complete. The dull pavement had been replaced with colored tiles, which sparkled in the sunlight; at each corner, bronze statues of hoplites stood guard. Thénai had sunk so much of its money into such projects, even at the expense of the military; and yet the border held, and the war had halted at a tenuous draw.

The House of Assembly, where Khloë entered, now boasted columns in the Megarine style, and a red-tile roof as bright as the City Square.

When she entered the foyer, she saw the gold statue of Phillipidēs, holding up the sphere of the earth on his shoulders, had been completed. It stood guard over the door, as she passed into the Council Chambers.

A woman stood there, dressed all in black, her hair and head covered in a cloth headdress which only revealed her face.

She was wizened and homely, wrinkled and bearing the signs of many long, hard years. She was speaking to the archon

Chairon.

As Khloë approached, she grew cold and tucked her shirt a bit tighter over her arms.

It was rude to wear sabers in the presence of an archon, but she had clipped them to her belt.

Chairon turned to face Khloë; Bat Zor did the same, and for the first time Khloë met her black eyes head on. Her gaze was dominating, her pupils black like onyx. She had seen eyes like those before, among mad sorceresses in the Amazonian Isles. This woman was a witch. Khloë was sure of it.

"This is Khloë the Amazon," said Chairon. "She saved us from the barbarian king."

"It was a group effort," said Khloë. She smiled. She offered her hand, but Bat Zor did not take it.

More than the character of her eyes, Khloë saw in her disdain.

This woman was not an Eloesian. She was not from this land; it was clear by her garb. And yet, did she harbor the same animus towards amazons? Did her people, too, tell of the war between amazons and humans? Did they spread rumors? Did they purvey false gossip? How else could Khloë explain that disdain?

"You come before a woman of rank, bearing swords?" Bat Zor said. "You were not taught well by your mother, Khloë the Amazon."

Perhaps the average woman would balk and scurry away in embarrassment. Instead rage welled up within Khloë. She sneered. "My mother was a warrior, not a pampered royal brat."

The derision in Bat Zor's eyes only grew. "This is the woman you were speaking of," she said to Chairon even as she glared at Khloë. "*This* is the hero you spoke of. *This* is the friend of Theron you praised so effusively."

"She is an Eloesian citizen," Chairon said, "and she has my

trust."

~

In the House of the Archon later that night, long after she'd skulked away in embarrassment, Chairon explained just who and what Bat Zor was.

In the center of government, Khloë's makeshift home, over a glass of red wine, Chairon spoke in hushed tones. "She is a sorceress, I am sure of it," Chairon said. The candlelight reflected in a dim glow against Chairon's clean-shaven face. The dark hall was so silent, Khloë could hear her own breath.

"I don't trust her," Chairon said. "She offered an alliance against the Kersican League. She offered it without anything in return. Tharta on our side… and yet we have made a pact with a demon. I do not know what she wants. There is no altruism in her body."

"Indeed," she said, and looked around the room, wondering if her eyes and ears were all around, if she—in her ground-level guest quarters—could somehow view them from a distance. "We should reject her offer."

"No." Chairon's eyes were pensive in the light of the candle. "We will accept their help. For the sake of our citizens… for the sake of our home. We can't let the Kersican League overcome us."

"We are at a draw." That was her best argument. A peace caused only by a military stalemate… an inability for one side to conquer the other. It was a recipe for eternal strife.

"I'm not happy with a draw," said Chairon.

Khloë looked down. "But I'm so afraid of her."

The next morning, Bat Zor and her retinue left Thénai's harbor on ships with purple sails. Those sails bore the four-pointed gold star of the southrons, not Eloesus' laurel wreath. The light of dawn had turned the sea a shade of pink. Khloë was glad to see her go.

But soon she would be back, more powerfully than before, with the weight of an army behind her. "Amara help us," she whispered. "Amara help the world."

THE WOODS OF GYGES, THENOA

It was night. The cicadas were singing. The heat of the day still lingered, and beads of sweat clung to Theron's skin.

Ropes were tied so tightly to his hands he feared that, if he moved even slightly, he feared a cut might open and he might bleed.

He was in a forest clearing, amid ancient oaks and cypresses. Torches burned, revealing the forms of Maids of Prophecy.

He knew these woods. He had been here before. These were the Woods of Gyges, in what used to be called Stygia.

He had been here before, yes. These woods were deeply familiar to him.

These trees had stood for centuries, these cypresses, these oaks covered in ivy, these ferns and grasses and mosses. What Phillipidēs had seen, Theron saw now. Nothing had changed over the eons.

He was tied to a stretcher, a device of torture banned in Thénai, what veterans of wars had called affectionately "the Yawning Nymph."

Bit by bit it would stretch his legs until they were broken or useless, or—at its maximum length—tear them out altogether.

The Maids of Prophecy gazed at him, smirking in self-satisfaction as they awaited his inevitable torture.

They had finally gotten him, they thought. Now, at last, the hero of the Southron War would fall.

Their leader, wearing a gown of white linen pulled a wooden lever.

The pain that jolted through Theron's body caused his veins to burn like fire. He cried out in agony. He could not bear this. He could not bear it at all.

"Where is the stygian water?" the woman shouted. "Where is the pool you drank from?"

"You're a madwoman!" he screamed. "You're insane!"

"You saw the future. You read a thread of destiny. Where did you drink from? Answer me! Where is this pool?" Her tone was biting.

Theron tried to scream something, but the pain overwhelmed him so much, all that came out was a gargle.

She pulled the lever.

Theron jerked and twisted so badly he bit his tongue. His mouth instantly filled with blood.

"Where did you drink from?"

"I never saw the future!" Theron tried to scream, but all that came out was "Saw… Future!"

"We are not fools!" the woman snapped. "We will let you live if you tell us what happened."

In his childhood, Theron had payed homage to the goddess Amara in her temple, offering the best of calves that could be bought in the market. In the temple he had been named; he had been anointed with oil. Where was Amara now? Where was the Mother? Where was the Virgin Queen of War?

She was dead!

"We will let you live!" the woman screamed. "The Oracle will let you live! Where is the Stygian water? Where is the pool you drank from? Tell us and we will spare your life!"

Tears of pain were trickling down Theron's cheeks. He could scarcely breathe. The sinews of his arms and legs were stretched so tight it felt they would burst at any moment. He cried out again in agony.

In the torchlight, he could see—across the clearing, near the brush, *Titan's Fist,* his club, lying unattended.

He cursed Amara. Where was she? He cursed Tyros. Where was he? The gods were dead, their thrones empty. All Theron had was himself, his hopes, his own strength.

The woman set her hand on the lever. Another shift would rip his arms apart. "Where is the pool you drank from?"

As he looked at the woman, dressed in white, her cool gaze, her pursed lips, her icy eyes, the pain in his limbs burst forth to anger. He clawed and stretched and twisted his arms. The rope hung tight. The lever was pulled.

The pain surged further. Theron screamed and wailed; he wept. He was losing control.

Some, like Khloë, thought him more than human. She believed he was a demigod. It was not so.

"Where is the Stygian water?" the woman snapped again.

If he had the answer, he couldn't speak it. He tried to say something, but all that came out was blubbering.

The woman approached. The night grew silent. The crackle of the torches and the chirps of the cicadas were calming to Theron, even as the pain coursed through his veins, even as the strands and sinews of his arms were stretched to their breaking point, even as his arms were separated from his shoulder bones. If he told this woman what she wanted, and she released him, he would still die.

"Please," he muttered to whatever god or spirit or demon could hear him, "save me…"

The woman held a cup up to his lips. Theron drank, finding it—to his surprised—filled with water. It was ice cold, refreshing pure to his lips, and he drank it all down—but the momentary relief brought the pain raging back into focus, and he let out another wail.

"Tell us," she said, and the pain will end.

A shadow came galloping out of the woods. In an instant an arrow had struck the woman in white, followed closely by a second.

Aigon the Centaur stood there, bow in hand, as the Maids of Prophecy turned and ran, screaming. They dispersed like the wind.

One by one Aigon cut Theron's binds. His limbs fell to his sides like jelly. He lost consciousness. The cool night air comforted him, ushering him into a deep sleep.

He awoke to screams. Aigon had fashioned together a great, raging fire. The wounded woman lay amid the flames, screaming, even as the fiery roar began to drown her out.

"Stop this!" Theron screamed. "Stop this madness!"

But he could not move his arms or legs. He could not sit up and force Aigon to do his bidding. Aigon was stoking the flames, even as his victim writhed and agony and slowly, was becoming silent.

"Stop this! I demand it of you!" His words fell on deaf ears.

There was no mercy in the centaur's eyes, only joy at her getting what she deserved.

But even if this is what she deserved, Theron didn't want her to have it.

Aigon continued fanning the flames.

When, in the morning, the fire had run its course, it lay in the golden sunlight as a pile of ashes. There was no trace of the woman left, only char.

Aigon had set Theron on a cot. He could move his limbs, but only with aches and pains. He strained to move them, but he could.

"Why did you do it, Aigon?" Theron said.

But he already knew the answer. Aigon had surely been

following him for days, keeping a distance but always standing guard. His act was one of anger and fury. In Theron's opinion it had been gratuitous.

Though he knew the answer, he asked the question again. "Why did you do it, Aigon?"

"You know," Aigon said, his giant form casting a long shadow in the morning light, "The Oracle was once kind to Phillipidēs. She turned on him, too."

Aigon had made him a breakfast of sorts—assorted mushrooms and berries scrounged from around the woods. His arms burned as he strained to eat them.

The pain had shaken him to the core, but the full extent of the "Yawning Nymph" had not been used on him. Aigon had saved him, just in time. His limbs were not broken. He could still shovel this measly breakfast into his mouth. Aigon had not bothered to wash the mushrooms; they were still caked, partially, in dirt. He spat them out.

"The Oracle killed Phillipidēs," Aigon said. "I must make sure it doesn't happen to you."

"Why?" Theron grumbled.

"You need to stay away from her," Aigon said. "You can't fight her. She will end you."

"You can't dissuade me."

"Look what happened!"

"I will end her," Theron answered, firmer than before.

In the light of dawn, the morning birds had begun to chirp. The oaks and laurels provided a green canopy even—as summer's onset progressed—the grass had turned a golden brown. The air around him was thick with a piney scent.

Against the tranquility, the Yawning Nymph was still there, behind him, a monstrous work of wood and iron. What devious mind invented it? Did amazons also create devices of torture, to inflict pain on their own… or was this only something humans did to one another?

"We should leave," Aigon said. "She knows where we are."

"And where would we go?"

"Far away."

Beyond the borders of Eloesus, beyond even far Isteros, a world unspoiled by humans could be found. Islands of civilization—the colonies—stood guard amid the wilderness, but all around them were deadly beasts and horrific forces of nature. Perhaps Theron could overcome them, but he would not go.

"I will kill the Oracle," said Theron. "I will end her. You can kill her with me, or you can stay behind."

With those words, he grabbed *Titan's Fist*. He walked off, out of the woods, expecting to go alone.

By the time he reached the road, the figure of Aigon hulked over him, trotting along by his side.

THE LAUGHING TRITON, THENOAN INLET

The ship cut like a dagger through the bright blue waters of the sea. The wind had been fortuitous, the weather sunny and exemplary. It had been two days since Gaia left Thénai, and her medicine had been unattended.

At night, when she slept on the deck, in full view of the stars, the apparitions of the demiurge failed to emerge. Perhaps he was lying in wait, when she was most vulnerable.

For now, she did not have to suffer the indignity of consuming night's eye.

And yet, holding on to the railing as the wind drove the ship along, she was not entirely well. They had recently passed Choros, where the treasury of the Kersican League lay protected among walls and fortifications. Despite the lack of nightmares, her sleep had been troubled, laced with fear of what might happen. She remained ill.

When her servants asked in concern, she answered bitingly. They would not understand. They would label her insane. They would tell her to go to Dys, to the Temple of Sollust the Healer, and lay down amid the sacred serpents until her mind was cured. Gaia knew from experience such sacred magic doesn't work. The gods had no power over the living, if they were real. Her best hope lay in apothecaries… in night's eye?

An island was coming into view. Palm trees lined its sandy shore. Beyond its coast were mountains covered in green cypresses and pine trees clinging to rock.

"Salitis ho!" a sailor cried.

They would stop at this island, "Salitis." For now, Gaia thought with dread, they would remain in the dominion of the

Thenoan League. They would remain behind enemy lines.

~

Salitis, to Gaia's surprise, had its own port and something like a town.

As the sailors tied the ship to the dock, an uneasy feeling came over Gaia, that something wasn't right.

This island was small, and if any population lived here it was impoverished, certainly unable to afford cargoes of perfume. Olive trees surrounded the town; why would they need to purchase oil?

Though Gaia was ill and exhausted, she knew she had to be ready. Something wasn't right, here. Something suspicious was at work.

When her servants surrounded her like a gaggle, anticipating the idea of finding an inn, she surprised them: "We have to leave this ship. We have to run. We won't be taking 'The Laughing Triton' to Thénai."

They looked at her as if she was mad. But it did not matter what they thought. They were the servants and she was the mistress.

~

Tired and weary, consumed with dread, Gaia walked throughout the town hoping to find the local inn.

In ancient days, before the advent of commerce and before wealth began to pour in from the colonies, there was no need for inns. When a traveler arrived in Thénai from abroad, common people invited them in for free lodging. Not so anymore. There was no trust, anymore. Strangers were viewed with suspicion. Everyone, naturally, looked out for their own safety and interests, worrying the lodger might take advantage of their generosity and then rob them blind.

In the village market, amphorae were being unloaded.

Olive oil, perfume—she no longer believed it. Gaia knew they'd be robbed or killed if they stepped foot on the ship again.

Her servant-girl Korë, wearing a headscarf, approached her. "Mistress," she said, "I fear there are no inns here. I know the journey is long, but Korthos—"

"Silence," Gaia snapped. "You think you know better but you don't."

Korë knew better than to talk back. She slinked away.

Gaia was growing faint. She needed to rest. The sleepless nights had begun to wear on her in full.

And yet, it was not until hours later, that the servants found lodging for Gaia.

In this rural island, marred by poverty, a rich man lived, on a hill outside of town. His name was Malechon.

"He raises horses," Korë said. "He owns the whole island. He wants to meet you."

COURTYARD, HOUSE OF THE ARCHON, THÉNAI

They had made a pact with a demon, against Khloë's wishes. Bat Zor was now their ally. With Chairon's blessing, they had fallen in league with a sorceress, all to break the stalemate between the Kersican and Thenoan Leagues.

It was daytime and the sun illuminated the red tile roof of Thénai's center of government.

Chairon and Khloë were seated on a table, amid the bubbling fountain. Summer had set in and the midday heat had not yet arrived. There was still time to bask in the brightness and light. Their talk had turned to their disagreement.

"I don't trust her either," said Chairon. "But for true peace to be achieved, Thénai must dominate..."

All around them, the sound of birdsong was evident. Nearby, a royal sunbird was perched on a pinebush, twisting its purple crest this way and that, searching for worms and bugs to eat. In less troubled times, such a sight would comfort her. Now Khloë was concerned for the Thenoan League; she was concerned for her city, for her world.

"I think the stalemate has worked out nicely," said Khloë. "There hasn't been any serious bloodshed in what? A fortnight?"

"There is more," said Chairon. His voice was laced with trepidation. "The Assembly held a vote last night."

Khloë had a sick feeling of what was coming.

"You've been selected to go to Thénai and see this alliance through."

It figured. Khloë was an amazon. She was expendable. All amazons are fearless, right? Caring not at all about safety, willing to throw away their lives in service of a greater goal?

And yet Khloë nodded her head. "Whatever is required," she said. "I'll go."

In a way it was surprising. Khloë was not a diplomat. She did not have a silver tongue.

But she had a great sense of duty—and she would do what others refused.

And who but her would agree to venture deep into enemy territory, to make an alliance with an ancient foe? Who else would dare to meet Bat Zor's cunning gaze and all it entailed?

Khloë would do what had to be done.

~

Before the sun rose the next day, Khloë was on the deck of a warship. A bevy of government servants and a battalion of hoplites would accompany her to these uncharted waters. As the representative of the Thenoan League, she'd try to strike a grand bargain with an old enemy. Who else could they expect to assume this monumental task?

On board *The Sea Eagle*, her entourage included fellow amazons. They were relegated to the most menial roles; but unlike in Korthos, they were given full rights and a reasonable ability to get ahead. Many of her amazon sisters manned the oars as the ship took off from the harbor. Others formed an auxiliary force to the hoplites, bearing glaives and wearing chakrams on their arms. Her decision to swear allegiance to Thénai and not Korthos had been one of her best. She had fully joined the other side; whatever was best for Thénai, she'd do.

These seas would carry her far away, to a place she'd never been, to a place where she didn't belong.

~

When Khloë stepped off the ship and onto Tharta's pier, she stooped over and retched over the railing. She had not suffered from seasickness very frequently, but this voyage had taken a lot out of her. It was the longest she'd been at sea, ten long days aboard a vessel. It was more than her landlubber body could bear.

On the pier, drifting in from the harbor, was the scent of pipesmoke. The smell reminded her of whenever southron traders came to Tigris to trade. Their long pipes would leave a scent long after they left. This was the very same scent.

The harbor was dirty, with garbage strewn carelessly along the piers and on the various twisting streets. Docked near *The Sea Eagle* were southron ships—dhows with lateen sails, colored various hues of rust and orange. Idling by the docks, amid a flock of seagulls flying overhead, men in turbans were unloading cargoes from ships.

This was no longer Eloesus. This was the southron world.

The greeting party was approaching: Thenoans in their blue capes and crested helmets were approaching, dozens of hoplites marching line-by-line. At their front was a woman dressed all in black, her wizened face a white spot amid her dark headdress. Bat Zor had been expecting them. Waiting, at any moment.

The sight of her unnerved Khloë and she wanted to run away and hide in the cabin; but for better or worse she was the leader of this expedition. If she showed fear, her inferiors would lose control as well, dooming their mission to disaster.

"Greetings!" Bat Zor cried.

Khloë bowed slightly.

"You are disarmed. An improvement, my sweet."

Khloë blushed at the mothering, insulting comment. Yes, she had left behind her sabers. It was rude of her to point it out.

But she had taken great pains in this endeavor, pains she didn't want. For the first time in her life, she had looked in the mirror. She had brushed and braided her hair. Instead of her familiar leather jerkin and vambraces, she had donned a gown of white silk.

It isn't me, she had mouthed to her reflection. *I am pretending.* She wasn't pretty enough for the braided hair or the silk gown. It embarrassed her to see herself like that. She was not a lady; she was not a diplomat. She was not a queen or an ambassador.

She was Khloë, who played with her sisters in the mud, and fought her friends with wooden swords before she could purchase a real one. She was Khloë, who knew since her girlhood that she wanted to fight and become a warrior, and see the world.

This was not her. And seeing Bat Zor's prying eyes, she felt all the more vulnerable, all the more pretend.

"I bring you greetings on behalf of the Thenoan League and its commander Chairon," Khloë said. She had rehearsed those words over the intervening days and nights at sea, just as she had rehearsed many more. She would play the part of a silver-tongued ambassador. She was sure she would fail.

~

The smell of pipes grew stronger as they passed through the harbor gates.

The streets of Tharta were a scene of lethargy.

In street corners and on porches, Thartans—both native and southron—smoked pipes.

There were still traces of Eloesus left—the red-tile roofs, the columns, the statues and the fountains—but it all was being subsumed in the king's Fharaization project. On a street corner, laborers were hoisting a statue up with rope; it depicted not a hoplite or a demigod but instead—in its bronze color—the twisted body of some southron god, with a bulging tongue and bugged eyes, three sets of arms and the lower body of a scorpion. These were not Eloesian gods; they were not Eloesian creations. This was one more sign of the extremes Gygax was taking the nation to, a sign of where he wanted things to go, a sign of what he wanted his people to become.

While Tharta withered and crumbled, ox-carts with marble slabs were regularly arriving to the palace, and hundreds of laborers were hard at work expanding the grounds.

"Gygax is expanding his harem!" said Bat Zor.

Harems. Multiple wives. A southron custom indeed. Khloë knew of amazons with many husbands, but custom demanded they be brothers. She was sure King Gygax had no such restrictions.

"How many wives does your son-in-law have?" asked Khloë.

"I lost count at one-hundred," Bat Zor said. "But my daughter sits above them all."

In Amazonia, polygamy was viewed as immoral and base. In Eloesus—at least before Gygax—it was illegal. In both societies, not long ago, the southron style of polygamy was abhorred.

There were hungry children with begging bowls near the palace gate. Their faces and bodies were gaunt, with skin stretched tight against those little bones.

What had Fharaization brought? Hunger. Sorrow. The smell of pipe smoke.

~

In a kingdom with so many queens, the palace had become a nursery. There were toddlers running around and nursemaids feeding infants. There were more children than Khloë could count, and they filled the courtyard; they filled the hallways and chambers. *Children, children, everywhere.* She almost tripped over one as they passed the vestibule.

Khloë's sister had two children, and could scarcely manage the challenge. She could not imagine the burden these hundreds of children imposed—and especially on the father they all shared.

She had read extensively about Gygax.

He was thirty-two years old, the son of a father also named Gygax—a father who had declared allegiance to the Fharese Empire and vowed to join, along with all his people, the southron world. What his father started, Gygax now rushed to completion. Gygax, the report had told her, "has banished all semblance of democracy in his city. He is an autocrat, a king with no check on his power."

~

The man sitting on the throne did not look thirty-two.

His eyes were glazed when they looked upon Khloë. There were wrinkles around his eyes and despite the sizeable gut he'd developed he seemed at the same time emaciated and weak. The stress of a dozen lifetimes seemed to weigh on him. This was an autocrat, a king; it was also a broken man.

The woman beside him had no such problems. On a smaller throne she sat, her face fresh and comely. She was pregnant.

Zubeida, her name was, the chief wife, the Queen of Tharta. She was much better dressed than the other wives and surely the recipient of all sorts of envy: wearing a purple brocade dress, a necklace of diamonds gleamed around her neck, and the rings which studded her fingers boasted rubies, emeralds and sapphires. Around her left arm was a gold band inset with onyx and carnelian. She was clearly favored; and, seated next to her ailing husband, a study in contrasts.

"I bring you greetings from the Thenoan League and its leader, Chairon," Khloë said once more. She had perfected the statement's tone. Perhaps she'd be insulted by Gygax's dead, dull look but he had all the signs of years of stress, brought on by his hundred wives and their bickering. Did he have a thousand children? Khloë wouldn't be surprised, judging by the number of young creatures running around.

Gygax's stare turned to a bitter glare. Suddenly Khloë remembered the gestures and moves she'd been trained for; before a king or queen, a lesser person must bow.

She dropped to her knees. "Your Majesty," she said, and her retinue followed, bowing down alongside her.

She bristled at the sycophancy of it. In Amazonia, a free warrior was loathe to bow to anyone. Amazonian emissaries abroad were thus, considered rude. And yet here Khloë sat, on her knees, groveling before the King and Queen of Tharta. There was no other way. She had to do this.

"Your emissary Bat Zor… had agreed to an alliance with the Thenoan League… against the Kersicans." Surely she was just repeating what Gygax and his queen already knew. But Zubeida stopped her.

"Bat Zor. My mother," she corrected her.

Obviously, Khloë wanted to say. But she held her tongue.

"For alliance…" Gygax's voice, though strained, carried loudly through the throne room's alcoves and ceiling. "You must pledge your loyalty to the King of Tharta and to the Golden Throne. 'Blood and earth is what I require.'" He was quoting something. "'Blood and earth…' 'Breath and water.'"

A man emerged from the shadows of the throne. Khloë saw by his white turban and embroidered robes he was a rich man, a southron, and likely a satrap or high government official. "We have prepared you rooms in the Water Nymph wing. You will be well cared for during your stay. I promise you this."

Something was afoot. Khloë could tell by the way they spoke, their tones, the way they gazed at her. They were plotting something… and by Amara, she'd uncover it.

HILL COUNTRY, THENOA

It was hard not to stand out when a centaur walked beside you.

Most had only seen centaurs in ancient paintings or decorating the pediments of temples. To have a living, breathing centaur walking beside you was to start a firestorm of rumor; and draw all the agents of the Oracle to Theron.

Therefore, Theron and Aigon agreed not to use the roads, or go anywhere where onlookers might see them.

As summer set in the hills had turned to gold under an oppressive sky. The sun burned down on them, driving away all water and moisture. They had not seen or heard any people in this forsaken place. Every once in a while a shepherd with his flocks would appear, but they kept far away.

Aigon knew this land; though centuries separated him from his time among mortals, and he called each landmark by a curious name, he knew exactly where to tread, exactly how to reach the bent Mount of Prophecy and eventually—with Theron—deal cold justice to the Oracle.

It was anyone's guess whether they'd succeed, and though Theron had been supremely confident of his eventual victory, Aigon—over fireside chats—had planted doubts in his mind.

"You do not understand her power," he had told him last night.

Up ahead, far above, in the sky, an eagle cast his shadow over the burning hills. It seemed the heat of the sun had snuffed all the life out of the hill country. A deer stood far away, near a dried up creek bed, huffing and puffing, panting for water. Theron's waterskins had grown too low for comfort. He feared this summer would turn all of Eloesus into a desert; but that's how it felt each summer, before the blessed cool of winter, and the rain.

Aigon motioned Theron to stop. He drew out an arrow and nocked it to his bowstring.

"You're kidding," Theron muttered. The deer was at least a hundred yards away. Not even Aigon could strike the deer from this far.

And yet he drew the bowstring back in a great arc and sent the arrow flying. It struck the deer, who stumbled off in an injured run.

Aigon took off after the deer at a gallop, as fast as any of Eloesus' best thoroughbreds. He had surpassed Theron's best expectations once again.

They would eat well tonight.

~

They stopped early that day. Theron watched as Aigon took out his stone knife and began dressing the deer, cutting out its intestines and unsavory organs. The smell wasn't something you could get used to or bear.

"There is no wood," Theron pointed out.

"It tastes good raw," said Aigon. "You would be surprised."

Eating raw meat was the sign of a barbarian or an Isteroi. But these were strange times, and strange circumstances.

As a young boy, Theron's mother told him a story about the centaurs, how they disrupted and ruined the wedding of the mythical King Targassos.

In those times—the so-called Archaic World—did Eloesians eat raw meat? Did they behave like the barbarians and savages that they now scorned? Who's to say the Eloesians of the archaic era weren't the same as Isteroi and whiteskin northerners?

To his great surprise, after Aigon had cut and fileted the

haunches of venison and handed one to Theron, the flavors that filled his mouth were pleasing. The raw meat was tender and moist. Spices and salt added flavor, but cooking or charring it took much of the meat's character away; Theron wondered if he'd ever set meat on a fire ever again.

"You do not know how lucky you are," Aigon said. "For me to have been following you. For the Maids of Prophecy not to know I was there. You are truly fortunate."

The words which Theron's torturer had used were percolating in his mind. "She said I 'drank Stygian water.' That I knew the future. What does she mean?"

"I don't know," Aigon answered. "The Oracle is a liar. When Phillipidēs came for her guidance, she told him she would protect him. Instead she betrayed him. She also told him to trust his lover Laodikē… and she mixed a poison for him."

Theron knew, as did everyone who listened to the epic song, that the temptress Laodikē had done him in. He had never known of his relation to the Oracle. Nor was that information included in any additional tale or ballad Theron had heard.

And yet here he stood, feasting with Theron: Aigon, the wisest of centaurs, Phillipidēs' tutor. He had waited in the mountains, hiding among the trees, keeping away from the affairs of mortals until this moment. Aigon had selected Theron as a new hero to tutor.

But could Theron ever measure up to Phillipidēs? His confidence in himself was unparalleled but even that seemed a stretch. Phillipidēs was revered across Eloesus; offerings and prayers were laid before his *herodium* in Tharta. Theron deserved no such thing. What had he done, in truth?

He had—according to the deceptive Maids of Prophecy— slain the avatar of Kronos. He had contributed in his own way to victory in the Southron War. No singer or minstrel would ever compose a song about such feats.

He had to earn his glory, his "imperishable fame." He had to venture to the Mount of Prophecy, and strike the Oracle dead where she stood.

In the wan light of the moon, Aigon ate the venison like an animal, tearing apart its sinews and flesh with his teeth.

"Stygian water," Theron said again. He had heard those words before, but they were foreign. He did not understand, truly, what they meant. "What is Stygian water?"

Aigon tossed the inedible remnants of his haunch of venison to the ground. His face was bloody. "In my time… when I lived among the mortals… Stygia was the greatest of the Eloesian kingdoms. Stygidos sat on the shore of a great lake.

"I remember when the being fell from heaven… a creature of light fell in battle and a piece of him fell into the water like a shooting star."

It seemed like he was reciting a poem, or the words from a song.

"It glowed for three years. The lake burned. Stygidos and its kingdom fell. The lake began to dissolve… but weapons were made. And whoever drank the water received supernatural gifts. Prophecy. Flight. True sight."

Theron thought he understood. But when had he predicted the future? When had he seen a premonition? It had never occurred. The Maid of Prophecy was mistaken. She had erred. If this is why the Oracle was after his life, she was either a fool, or a liar.

"If you had truly drunk Stygian water," Aigon said, "you'd be lighting up the night. I could see by your glow…"

"So they lie… it was an excuse to torture me."

"Centuries have passed since that time," Aigon said. "The Maids of Prophecy, maybe even the Oracle herself, could have forgotten. When you prophesied, that was the only explanation they knew."

"Prophesied," Theron scoffed. "I've never prophesied. They've gone mad. Or they're liars. Or both."

To his surprise, Aigon's eyes reflected impatience, perhaps even disbelief. Did he truly take the Oracle's word over his own? Did he not share Theron's hatred? Did he not take Theron's side?

"I'm sure you're right," Aigon said. "You don't recall. You don't remember… But—"

"No," Theron snapped. "I did not prophesy. I can't see the future. If I could see the future, I'd never have been captured. I would have run from the Yawning Nymph. I would have holed up in Thénai." The memory of that pain lingered with him, hovered over him, haunted him. At night, his arms and legs still ached. He braved his way through it, but he still struggled to sleep and function. If he was a prophet he would never have taken that first step out of Lion's Gate. He would have accepted the kingship which he did not want. He would have remained safe in Thénai's walls.

He would have lived his life thinking only of avoiding the Mount of Prophecy's unholy grip. Now, with the memory of that injustice, the hatred had consumed him, and vengeance was the only thing that mattered… to see *Titan's Fist* strike the Oracle dead, to cast down every pillar of her temple, to cut the head off her serpent. He would risk capture for the hope of it. He would risk pain, degradation, even the Yawning Nymph. Nothing mattered except the delivery of justice. He would risk destruction to see it done.

"How far are we to the foothills?" said Theron.

The land rose long and laboriously until it reached the lofty meadows of Themuria and its Mount of Prophecy. The journey would be as deadly as any Theron had ever taken. But it was worth it. The hope of justice was worth it.

"A week, perhaps," said Aigon, "until the ground rises and the air turns cold."

SALITIS, ISLE OF SALITIS

Hiring a horse and carriage, Gaia's servants prepared a comfortable seat for her with pillows and blankets. Then they left the town of Salitis on the similarly-named isle, and began—with their guide—what they were told was a long journey.

The owner of the Isle of Salitis, who fancied himself a prince, was a "partisan of the Thenoan League, but open minded"—thus said the guide.

Gaia's Korthian affiliations did not bother him; rather, they intrigued him and "further cemented the notion that he had to meet her."

It was sunset when the carriage left, and the mixed woods and scrub brush of the Isle of Salitis was painted in red and gold. All around them were the outlines of black mountains, shrouded in smoke. Laurel trees had sprouted up along the road. But everywhere, there was silence. Everywhere, there was abandonment. Gaia heard no birdsong, just the grinding of the carriage wheels, and the gentle breeze. Just yards from the town of Salitis, everything had evaporated into arboreal solitude. There were no animals, no birds, just shadows.

The guide, sitting in the carriage with them, couldn't seem to stop talking. "Prince Malechon built his house as far away from his subjects as he possibly could."

Hours later, long after the sun had set beneath the sea, when the night was dark and only the moon and stars offered light, the carriage made a turn off the dirt path. Gaia awoke from her half slumber. Up in the sky a colony of bats was circling. A feeling of dread fell over Gaia as she beheld Malechon's villa. Its isolation was supreme. Built near the shore, the only signs of its presence was candlelight filtering in through the windows. It was an island in the inky blackness of the countryside.

As they turned down the roadside which wound its way to the villa, Gaia saw—despite the darkness—many yards of fencing, and the shapes of horses in the distance. It was as the villagers of Salitis said: "Malechon loves horses more than people."

Malechon was wealthy, no doubt world-wise. He was of Gaia's class, and no doubt shared many of her values.

And yet, as she approached this villa, which was isolated and alone, a sense of dread was building, a growing fear she could not escape. She hoped the sight of Malechon would ease her fears, if—beyond the dim lit windows—the villa hid warm and welcoming décor.

Servants greeted them at the gates of the villa. Their cloaks were as dark as the night landscape around them. Bearing torches, they waited as Gaia and her servants exited the carriage. Then they led their vehicle away.

VILLA OF THE SWORD, ISLE OF SALITIS

Gaia's stomach turned when she first met the owner of the island, the one who called himself a "prince."

Malechon was pale for an islander, extraordinarily tall and thin. His brown hair was patchy and mixed with silver. He wore a long robe, scarlet-colored, and a black rope belt which cinched it over him. "Greetings," he said.

"Greetings," Gaia answered, and her voice betrayed a tremble. She was glad she had Korë here, and male servants such as Philemon whom she trusted. Between her recurrent nightmares, Malechon and the Villa of the Sword, her stress was eating her away. She would not rest easy here.

She should have taken the ship on to Korthos. Her paranoia had dissuaded her; her terrible dreams and premonitions had not saved her, but instead pushed her here, to this point, to terror. Paintings were hung along the walls, one of Ansolon the founder of democracy and the other of Hordo his wife. A statue was in the vestibule, of Nix the mother of witchcraft and healing knowledge. She was painted in lifelike detail, with a dog beside her and an owl perched on her shoulder.

Nix was worshipped in Korthos, but only with great terror. As the mother of sorcery, worship was done with care; and though she occupied a prominent place in the city's religious life, she was also the fodder of scary tales. To have her protection was to defend yourself with a dark force.

Gaia reminded herself that such statues were common even in her home city, that—though the torchlight cast a long shadow against this likeness—invoking her protection was nothing sinister.

The statue's face was lifelike, painted gray and wizened, so detailed it had the shape of boils and wrinkles etched into the underlying marble. The statue's eye sockets were affixed with bright yellow tiger's eye gems. It was not what Gaia wanted to see when she first entered the villa; it was not what would comfort her in her fear.

Her heart began pounding, and soon her hands were clammy and cold, layered with sweat. She had made many mistakes over her long life. Would this be the biggest?

Behind the Villa of the Sword was a guest house with a private garden, looking over the cape. The stars reflected brightly in the sky and the sound of the waves rushing into the rocky shore formed a constant backdrop.

Some of her stress washed away with the sound of the waves, until she headed to her chamber and looked in her mirror.

She looked terrible. She was paler and thinner than before. There were bags under her eyes from lack of sleep. Stress lines appeared on her forehead, stress lines which had become permanent marks, which nothing could mend.

Nightmares are harmless, people said. But these nightmares were killing her. If she did not cure them, she'd die.

She set the tin of night's eye on the bedside table.

Malechon had offered his hospitality. He had given her a bed fit for a queen, with silk curtains and a thick purple blanket. Surely he could be trusted. Surely Gaia's terror would be restricted to her dreams alone.

Before dinner, she powdered her face and reddened her lips. She had a show to put on.

Malechon was married—Gaia had seen the figure of a

woman in the courtyard as she walked to dinner. And yet she was alone with Malechon save the chefs and servants. His stare was unnerving, but Gaia endured it for her own sake. Malechon would provide her with information. He'd know when a ship was due to leave. Wouldn't he?

"You wear cosmetics," said Malechon, "but I can see something is eating you, Gaia of Korthos."

The statement was unwelcome. Gaia knew she was on the brink. She did not need this stranger reminding her, this stranger whom she didn't trust, this stranger whose gaze was dark and black, whose emaciated form was reminiscent of the dead.

"Tell me, what is it?" Malechon said. "What troubles you?"

Gaia gritted her teeth together in frustration. "Well, I'm in Salitis," she said. "I was hoping to be in Korthos by now. But I thank you for your hospitality."

On the door leading to the kitchen, a protective amulet was hung, with purple and blue feathers, a metal disc and a clay-fired skull. Invoking Nix's protection, Malechon was making his religious views clear. Gaia had seen such charms before, in homes in Korthos—even among the wealthy and educated. She had scorned such charms as superstition, the product of a feeble mind.

But perhaps a charm was what she needed. A token of Nix's protection. Yes. Priests say the gods are greater than demons. If so, Nix was stronger than the demiurge.

Her exhaustion was causing her to think crazy things. The gods were statues, nothing more. The haunting of her dreams was surely a product of her long paranoia, the rigors of navigating Korthian high society.

But if it was just paranoia, why did it seem so real? And why had the supposed hallucination led her to the Gauntlet, within the fires of Mount Kronos?

Perhaps she had imagined finding the Gauntlet as well.

She needed to rest. She needed to regain her sanity. She needed to achieve peace of mind. But how could she, with the threat of nightmares?

Malechon was staring at her, examining her.

For a while they sat in silence. Then the servants came in, bearing platters of food: squid, breaded and fried; clams and mussels drizzled in olive oil and spices; tuna and mackerel and dolphinfish; and candied lemons sparkling with sugar. The servants filled their goblets of wine.

It was far too much for Gaia to eat, especially in her weakened, frazzled state. Still she directed her servants to give her a few clams. It was all she could eat, and the least—she'd guess—upsetting to her stomach.

The wine was dark and fruity, and calmed her somewhat. Perhaps she had it in her to relax. Perhaps, if she breathed deeply, if she relaxed her muscles…

She awoke with a start, seconds later. She was dozing off. She had not slept well in weeks. Wasn't it to be expected?

"You aren't well," Malechon said, stating the obvious.

"No, I am not."

When she told him about her dreams, about the recurrent nightmares gripping her, she left out the ugly details of the demiurge lest he curse her like the priests did. She did not want condemnation for "trafficking with demons." This had never been her choice.

Out of the portal to another world, the ash-colored hand had pointed to her. The demiurge had chosen Gaia; Gaia had not chosen the demiurge.

"You need to rest," Malechon said. "Even if you fear the nightmares. Your lack of sleep is destroying your body."

She had done the demiurge's bidding; she had recovered

his Gauntlet and placed it on the arm of Rogon. Then, he had promised, he would relinquish the grip he had on her. He would let her sleep, he said. And then he proved every word he spoke was a lie.

"I can't sleep," said Gaia. "I won't." This sickness was better than the sight of the demiurge, emerging from the shadows.

She picked apart and ate the clams, which were seasoned artfully with oil and spices. The heartier stuff she would not touch, even as Malechon voraciously gobbled down his mackerel and fried squid.

When the evening had grown late, and her wine cup— thrice-filled—had become empty, Gaia said, "I think it's best that I go rest."

Malechon nodded. He had eaten all the squid and fish, by himself. His thinness was an enigma. "My wife Hora has a garden. Perhaps there are some herbs that will allow you to sleep."

"Is there a ship coming soon?" Gaia said. "I must get back to Korthos."

Her voice betrayed her discomfort. Yet Malechon's gaze only grew more intense. "Perhaps," he said. "We will have to see. Ships often draw near the cape to fish. Who knows? One may be headed to Korthos."

It was late, perhaps past midnight, and yet—when Gaia left the feasting hall—Malechon's wife Hora was in the courtyard, watering a tangle of purple flowers. The moon reflected its white glow in the central fountain.

She was singing some inscrutable song, in a language Gaia didn't recognize. She wore a hooded cloak, and a veil over her mouth. In one hand she watered the flowers; with the other she was dropping some glittering substance. Her face was mostly covered;

but her eyes were dark and black, inky orbs which glinted white in the moonlight. Beyond the columns, on another door, there was another charm of Nix, a feathered wreath with a skull and two crossed swords. Was she the source of Malechon's household devotion? Did she revere the Queen of Sorcery? Did Hora honor She of the Silvered Sword?

When Hora turned to look at Gaia, Gaia panicked and took off toward the guest house at a sprint.

When she reached the inner chamber, her servants had started a fire and were sitting on the floor and on couches, laughing and joking with each other.

They had prepared her bed.

Gaia lay under the covers for a while, trying not to fall asleep, but she was too exhausted. Eventually she lost the will to stay awake; and drifted off into a deep, deep slumber.

She awoke, as she expected, in the middle of the night, paralyzed, ice-cold, clammy.

"Leave this isle!" the demiurge's shadowed form snapped. His eyes burned like red beacons. "Leave this isle, thou knave, and return to Korthos! Leave and go home, at once!"

By the time he left, Gaia had awoken once more, in the middle of the night.

Her servants were sleeping on the floor together, before the dying embers of the fire. Their faces were happy, restful, and at peace.

How she envied them. She would give up all her riches, all her titles, all her properties and all her gold and jewels just to sleep like they did—just to rest in peace.

She wept at the sight of them, sleeping snugly on the floor. What she wouldn't give to be them—to sleep in peace, even as a servant.

She'd forgotten the night's eye, in a tin beside her bed. It was her last hope.

She headed back to her chamber. She smeared the prickly powder across her gums. She waited.

When she awoke it was a bright sunny day. She was bound up, in the villa's courtyard, screaming. Her struggle against the ropes had rubbed her arms and legs raw.

"What happened to me?" Gaia screamed. "What happened?"

Her servants were glaring at her.

Malechon loomed over her. Hora, no longer wearing a veil or hood, was putting pressure on her arms, trying to keep her down. "We found you naked, in the fields."

Gaia flushed in embarrassment. She had been covered in a cloth.

How stupid she was to listen to that apothecary. How stupid she was to believe his recommendation, that night's eye, somehow, would cure her nightmares—nightmares that were not natural, but instead the product of a dark curse.

She was ashamed. She was embarrassed. She still screamed like a madwoman. She screamed because of the way they looked at her; she screamed because of the way they would look at her, not just today but in the days and weeks and years ahead.

WATER NYMPH WING, ROYAL PALACE, THARTA

"The southrons are making outrageous demands," said Teucer, Khloë's advisor, in the safety of their private chamber.

"Southrons," Khloë said. "You mean Thartans."

"What's the difference?" Teucer answered.

He had a point.

But Khloë wasn't sure what the archon wanted. Did he truly want Khloë to cut her hands, to offer the Thartans "blood and earth"—to offer fealty and not alliance? When she came here, offering terms of agreement and unity, she thought they would be partners, coequal in strength. Now Gygax demanded fealty, obeisance to the King of Tharta, not the trust and effort of an ally.

Did Chairon want Khloë to cut her hand, to grab earth and smear her hand on Tharta's civic altar? Even Teucer didn't know.

"I don't think we have a choice," said Khloë. "We can't go home empty-handed. I'll make the offering." Teucer probably thought Khloë would never do such a thing, that she had too much honor and martial dignity. After all, Khloë had told of her life in Amazonia, the battles, the wars, the ambushes.

Would a warrior like Khloë stoop to such degradation? Yes, she would. She had a duty to serve Thénai, not herself.

"Then go."

~

It was three days later when the ceremony began.

A battalion of hoplites marched with her along the main road, and civilians had gathered along the path to watch. Her stomach turned at the thought: this event had been widely broadcast, showing the Thenoan League's deference to Tharta. She questioned herself again, whether this is what Chairon would have wanted.

She had come for an alliance. She had received humiliation.

Behind her a woman dressed in black was beating a gong, forming a gloomy rhythm as they marched along the way.

Indeed, gloom seemed to have overtaken Tharta. Amid the crowd, Khloë couldn't make out a single smile. This was not a celebration; it was a funeral.

Perhaps it was Gygax; perhaps it had always been like this. Tharta was a city of few smiles and no laughter.

The gong rang again as they passed through Royal Tharta Gate.

Beyond, gathered in a crowd, was a waiting party.

That party included the king, Gygax, in a purple robe and a sunray crown; his chief wife Zubeida; and her mother, the ambassador Bat Zor. Bat Zor bore a knife, which gleamed in the sun. Her face was that of a crone, contrasting sharply with her black headdress; and in her dark eyes there was a gleam—a green speck, as she gazed upon her victim.

When Khloë arrived, her heart was racing and she was perspiring like mad. This was merely a ceremony, a symbolic ritual. It was not binding. And yet, she trembled, thinking this would somehow touch her soul. To say this was degrading was an understatement; and yet she stooped down and grabbed a handful of sun-dried earth, mixed with grass. She reached out her right arm and watched as Bat Zor took her knife and sliced, splitting skin and drawing blood.

She mixed the blood and earth together until it had turned to crimson mud. She said, "Let's go."

The gongs played as they made their way down the streets of Tharta, past the palace and up to the High City where the Temple of Alabastros stood.

High above, soaring over the city, the temple loomed, a masterwork of marble.

The stone of the temple was blinding white. The shingles of its rooftops radiated. Here was the home of Alabastros, Lord of the Sky, favored of kings, who alone could wield the thunderbolt. No temple in Eloesus was as brilliantly-colored; no temple in Eloesus so deserved its place among the clouds.

When she entered the vestibule, she kicked off her sandals. This was holy ground, even if it was foreign.

Beyond a colonnade, in an open hall, was the image of Alabastros: a statue thirty feet tall, colorless, the image of an old man kneeling over, carrying a spear of lightning.

Before the image was an altar, covered in blue cloth. Behind the statue, and above it, on the roof, scenes of clouds were painted, and cupids dancing among them with their miniature bows.

Not all things were southron. Some things remained sacred. The ancient god of Tharta was one of them.

In a world where culture—by decree of the king—was being intentionally destroyed, this edifice remained in place, this sacred home for the image of Alabastros. Some things Thartans could not let go of.

But how long before this holy statue was replaced with a southron monstrosity, with the head of a jackal?

For now, it remained in place.

Khloë approached the throne with Gygax's party and a crowd of civilians watching.

Fealty. Fealty to Tharta. Obeisance. Groveling.

No.

She would not do it.

She turned, and let the dirt, caked with blood, slip to the marble floor.

"I'm sorry," she said.

A look of outrage overtook Gygax and his party's faces.

Khloë held firm. "I came as an equal partner, as an ally in the fight against Kersica.

"We are either equals… or we go our separate ways." Khloë could feel a fight coming on. She knew the bloodsport well. She had kept her sabers on board the ship; she was utterly helpless.

"Then to prison you go," Gygax said.

Khloë heard Tharta had the most humane prisons in Eloesus, even bragged about it. Still, it was a life she would not tolerate. "No."

When a hoplite rushed her, bearing swords, she was ready, kicking him hard in the breastplate until his sword went flying. In mid-flight she grabbed it by the handle and rushed forward. The hoplites and Gygax's party fled in a panic.

She did not know this sword. Its weight and balance was foreign to her. Yet her skill had driven them all away.

"I declare war!" shouted Gygax, breathless. "I declare war on the Thenoan League!"

Perhaps it was best that way.

FOOTHILLS, THENOA

It was weeks since they left Thénai, and slowly but surely the ground was growing hillier and rockier. They approached, now, the Sky Mountains, the very roof of the world. That is where Theron's prey lived, hiding away in a mountain fastness. She awaited justice, justice at the end of *Titan's Fist*. Only gods knew if he could deliver it.

He uttered a prayer to Amara under his breath. If only she could provide him a sword of fire, and a mirror shield, like the hero Stratemon. He laughed at the thought. He only had his own strength, and his own wit, to see him through the day.

Following Aigon, they had spurned the roads, fearing the sight of a centaur would draw the attention of the Oracle and her maids.

The air was growing thinner, and a cold wind was blowing. In the distance, seemingly close but impossibly far away, were snowcapped peaks. There were many miles to go in this trek, many arduous climbs and tiring hikes.

More often than Theron wanted to admit, he'd thought of asking Aigon, "Can I ride on your back?" After all, he looked to be part stallion. But Theron had too much pride for that. These exhausting hikes, these rigorous climbs—they strengthened his body, they expanded his fortitude. By the time they reached their destination—having spurned the road and gone about the most treacherous way—Theron could face any foe. He could fight any battle.

This high up, the forest was thick and streams of water flowed abundantly down the hills. At all intervals, deer scattered away in fright, hares bounded away and squirrels skittered up treetops. Humans avoided this place due to the snow and the rugged terrain, but it was a bountiful land. In the days since they'd begun their climb, they hadn't gone hungry; Aigon, expert with the bow, faster than the deer themselves, always managed to find some quarry. Each night, after the exhausting climb, there was plentiful wood to start a fire.

That night, they stopped beside a brook. Aigon immediately got to work, gathering kindling for the campfire.

Theron had grown grimy and dirty after all these days. He unslung the lionskin from around his head and headed off into the woods.

In a thicket, in a deep part of the brook, Theron removed his clothes to bathe.

The ice-cold water took his breath away as he slowly inched deeper. As the water coursed across his bare skin he began to shiver, but he continued stepping deeper and deeper, into the silt, into the mud. His heart pounded as the icy waters covered him, washing away the grime of many days' travel. Breathless, he scrubbed away the dirt layered on his skin and beneath his fingers. He dipped his head into the cold water and ran a hand through his dripping-wet hair.

Water is good for the soul, he thought, and though the brook was freezing cold he remained, allowing it to cleanse him and restore his body's balance. He could not bear the temperature for long, but he'd remain as long as he could. He breathed deeply as the sun began to set over the woods, and the sky turned to reds and golds.

He shut his eyes, and sensed danger coming; he did not know how, or why. But a sense of vulnerability came upon him; unclothed, with *Titan's Fist* back at camp, he had reason to worry.

Naked he waded to shore. Before he got to his clothes he saw a shadow darting through the woods, toward the camp.

"Aigon!" Theron shouted. "Look out!"

When he reached camp, still not fully clothed, a fire was roaring, and Aigon stood there, bloodied, his saber dripping crimson. At his feet was a creature Theron had never seen before, a scaly monstrosity with a snake's tail and a cobra-like head.

"What is that?" Theron cried, aghast.

Its snake-tail was still slithering.

It was larger than Theron; now dismembered, he could make out little except the reptilian features of this aberration.

"What is that?" Theron shouted again, panic welling up within him.

"I've seen this creature before," said Aigon. "But not in centuries. This too is a servant of the Oracle. We have to be on our way. They've found us."

A horn blew in the distance, a war-horn. They were close, closer than Theron had imagined. This serpentine monstrosity had sniffed them out.

Without asking, Theron scooped up his bag and *Titan's Fist*, and hopped onto Aigon's back, who took off at a gallop. They left the camp behind, together with its comforts. They had escaped death by a knife's edge. Tomorrow, perhaps, they'd not be so lucky.

~

High up in the mountains, in the shelter of a cave, Aigon and Theron huddled together amid the freezing cold and bitter wind. They were alive and unharmed, but just barely escaping death.

"What was that?" Theron asked, shivering. His breath was

turning to fog. "Tell me again."

"I was born long after the Old Dominion fell.

"But I remember hearing a story… that the Ruined Temple where the Oracle lives was once called the Temple of Time."

And what does that have to do with that monstrosity, Theron wanted to ask. But instead he kept silent, wanting to hear Aigon's hard-won wisdom, wisdom which he had accumulated over centuries.

"Perhaps… that creature… perhaps it had something to do with it. I swear—before it went after Phillipidēs… I had seen the image of it somewhere, on a mural, or carved into stone…"

Outside the cave, it was pelting freezing rain.

Theron said another prayer, that the rain would cease, that the clouds would part, that the sun would shine.

Theron looked beyond the hills, and saw the bent shape of Mount Hylea. They were closing in.

THE PROFITEER

Quicksilver and mercury, tin and bronze—Agathion had purchased all those and more.

King Gygax had fallen in love with his automatons, the birds which flew across the room and cuckooed, the warrior with shield and sword who lurched across the room on his own. Each one costed a talent or more. And they costed him only a half dozen *doukon*.

Soon he would be a rich man. Build King Gygax a bronze menagerie… two talents. Build King Seres an automaton throne… three talents.

He could live in a palace!

Who cared that they would take fifty years to build?

HIGH CITY, THÉNAI

She had come to make an ally out of Tharta; she had returned with two enemies, the Kersican League and Eloesus' most powerful city.

Chairon, looking over the city below, put a hand over Khloë's shoulder. "Do not worry," he said. "We will survive."

Khloë wished she was that optimistic.

"We asked for an alliance… not fealty. I'm glad you didn't give it to him. You know, he is a pervert…"

Pervert or no, Gygax's personal predilections did not bother her. She, and the Thenoan League, had made a fearsome enemy in that incestuous monarchy and, above all, in Gygax's mother-in-law Bat Zor.

They could hold out against the Kersican League for as long as their walls and their navy held strong. But could they hold out against Tharta, the richest and greatest city in Eloesus, and the black eyes of Bat Zor?

Below her many fathoms, the citizens of Thénai were laughing and going about their daily business. Did she have responsibility for any disaster to come? She despaired at the thought, of harming anyone in this city, this city she'd grown to love. No, they had not always fully accepted her; but she was still alive, and according to city records she was one of the Thenoans. She had made an offering to the city gods. She had been washed, and anointed. Once she had been an amazon, but now she was a Thenoan—and perhaps the most powerful one of all?

She hoped an amazon, an outsider, had not spelled out their doom. She uttered a prayer to Amara, though her priesthood was no longer here.

It was late in the day, and the midday sun was bearing down on Khloë, when a horn blew from below, a horn whose melody and timbre she recognized, calling all the government to the House of Assembly for a meeting.

She had anticipated spending the evening in peace, in the coolness of the night air, perhaps with a glass of wine handy. It was not to be.

In the Assembly, with the two-hundred demiarchs gathered, one of the Strategoi stood there, his blue tunic festooned with medals of service. A leather belt cinched his leather leggings, and hanging from the belt was a curved saber, the kind of saber that admirals used. A military man had come, obviously, with news.

"War broke out between the Kersicans and the Korthians yesterday," said the Strategos.

The news rushed through the room like a good wind; demiarchs smiled. One clapped.

A divided League would fall. A divided League would rupture and break.

"Now is the time to make our move!" Khloë answered him. The Free and Democratic Army of Thénai was meant for this moment.

A garrison at the fort of Bos stood on Thenoa's border, locked in a tenuous truce with the Kersican army on the other side. Perhaps it was time to break that stalemate.

It took seven days of arguing and debate, sometimes with hot tempers, before all demiarchs and representatives from the tributary states agreed: "Enough of the deadlock," said the chief demiarch. "This body demands that Chairon send his armies across the border and engage the Kersicans in war."

Not long ago, fighting the Kersicans—the greatest soldiers of Eloesus, who trained their whole lives for war—would be considered suicide. Now Thénai was newly confident; victory did not seem impossible.

"Khloë." Chairon turned to her. "You will lead this fight."

Would the Free and Democratic soldiers respect her? A woman? An amazon?

Only time would tell.

SHRINE, VILLA OF THE SWORD, SALITIS

Dressed only in a white shift, Gaia stooped before the image of Nix and raised her hands.

She did not want to do this. She did not believe in, nor did she seek, Nix's power.

But Hora, wife of Malechon, garbed in a purple cowl, had insisted Gaia seek healing here. "Night's eye won't save you," she had told her. "Only the goddess can."

Gaia had succumbed to Hora's demands, hoping it would shut her up. The Grey Lady, She of the Silvered Sword, whatever they wanted to call her—was a story and nothing more, a creation of an imaginative mind.

The image lay before her on an altar, a figurine of silver, depicting a crone in a hooded cloak. A green candle and a white candle burned on either side of it. Above the altar, against the wall, was a sword forged of silver.

And yet, if She of the Silvered Sword was here, Gaia could not sense her like Hora claimed to. The columns and etchings of the shrine were cold, dead marble. Gaia was as empty and fearful here as she had been in her private chamber. And yet she continued to raise her hands. She shut her eyes and repeated the words which Hora had told her: "Heal me, Mother of Wisdom… Take from me the curse of the demiurge. Spurn his grasp over me. Heal me. Uplift me."

Perhaps she had spoken the words wrongly, or in an improper tone. Hora was looking at her sternly, tut-tutting like a paedogogue. She walked to an alcove, and from a jar produced a handful of purple flowers.

She placed the flowers in Gaia's hand. She knelt down

beside her. She whispered. "Here, take a deep sniff."

The scent was overpowering, clearing her sinuses instantly. Her nose dribbled almost instantly; her throat cleared up. She became dizzy. She handed the flowers back to Hora, coughing.

"Now say it again, clearer," Hora said, "and *believe* it."

She laughed at the thought of it. How could she force herself to believe something? She, and her family, had never given much consideration to temples and rituals. Growing up, it had been a civic duty and nothing more… a way to gain the respect of her peers in Korthos, a way to participate in the city's life.

But to actually believe in the goddess before her? The crone, who could heal dark maladies? The figment of imagination whom the desperately sick turned to?

All right. She would try. She told herself Nix was real, that she had true power over the world, that she truly lived in a place called Paradise, that she really had anything to do with this world, and the ability to cure Gaia's disease, that she could truly wrest her from the haunting of the demiurge.

"Heal me, Mother of Wisdom," Gaia said, and she impressed herself by sounding sincere. "Take from me the curse of the demiurge. Spurn his grasp over me. Heal me. Uplift me."

Hora grabbed hold of Gaia's lip. There was an angry look to her old eyes. "You sound cheeky."

Perhaps she could sense her serious doubts. This would not help. This would not save her.

And so she fell prostrate before Nix's image. She shouted, "Heal me, Mother of Wisdom! Take from me the curse of the demiurge! Spurn his grasp over me! Heal me! Uplift me!"

Apparently she pleased Hora, because she remained silent while Gaia cowered.

And when she finally sat up, she did feel better, albeit marginally; and for a brief instant, the thought of the coming night didn't dominate her thoughts.

Hora withdrew to a separate room and returned with a goblet. "Ceremonial wine," she said, "Take a drink."

The wine was bitter and laced with caustic herbs. Gaia managed to swallow it, nonetheless, albeit with a grimace. She handed the goblet back to Hora, still puckering.

And despite her complaints, when she left the shrine she did feel better, better than she'd felt in days.

That evening, amid the constant rush of the waves, Gaia and Hora went horseback riding. Gaia picked out a white mare and Hora a silver. Together they left the confines of a fence and headed out, up toward the mountains. Up an old path, through the pines and cypresses and scrub brush, they wound their way higher and higher, toward the cloudless sky.

Gaia had been here, in Malechon's villa, for only a week, but she had grown close to Hora. Hora, it seemed truly cared about Gaia's plight and sincerely wanted her to recover. She was like a physician, a physician who took more stock in rituals and prayers than in medicine and surgery. For better or for worse, Hora was fixated on Gaia's problems, and intent on solving them. She had a good heart; but could she deliver?

As they approached the summit, Gaia saw something which caused her to gasp and nearly fall off the saddle: a thing like a scarecrow, made of straw and sackcloth, in the shape of a crone—bulging chin, bug eyes and all. "What is that?" she cried. Her fear surprised her, at this inanimate object, which could do no harm.

And yet its bug eyes, crafted of white stone, without pupils or irises—its wild hair, made of straw—was just lifelike enough to give Gaia a throe of panic. And as they progressed, more of these creations appeared, lining the path.

"They are Nix's likenesses," said Hora. "They stand guard and protect from evil."

The more Gaia saw of Nix, the more she learned of her, the more it seemed the goddess herself was evil, dark-hearted and cruel. If anything, these likenesses cemented the thought. And yet, sandwiched between these creations on either side of the road, her fear of them banished thoughts of the demiurge and the coming night. Could Hora instill faith in Gaia, and cause her to believe? Gaia had her doubts, but Hora was close to making it happen.

At last, the path opened up into a clearing, and there, just beneath the summit, was an outdoor shrine.

An altar lay there, hewn from rock and covered in a blue cloth. Pews were behind it, carved of wood; and the whole of the shrine was marked with a border of stones. More faith-healing perhaps. Maybe, at last, it would do some good. In the past two days, she had no nightmares. Perhaps, if Gaia had faith, her run of luck would continue.

"Here is the final ritual," said Hora.

Gaia should have known this was not a mere horseback ride. If there was a more fervent devotee of Nix, Gaia did not want to meet her.

Gaia dismounted and, according to Hora's instructions, knelt down before the altar and stretched her hands upon it.

In the forest ahead, there was a small shed. Hora entered, and returned with a censer, and a scourge.

When she had lit the censer, and the smell of incense filled the clearing, Gaia's head began to ache. The smoke billowed out, clouding her vision. She entered a gray world, and there—amid the darkness—was Nix, holding the censer.

An old hag, she was, wrinkled, with sparse hair. Her teeth were fangs, like a shark's. Her eyes glowed yellow amid the incense, with the censer she was holding. She was laughing, cackling, consumed with madness. She drew closer and though Gaia wanted to run, she was paralyzed. Fear greater than anything she'd felt with the demiurge consumed her. Nix touched Gaia's chin with her bony finger, and Gaia screamed. She yearned for the demiurge. Never again would she fear the night. Never again would she fear her dreams.

~

It was the next day, and Malechon announced a ship was coming to take Gaia and her party to Korthos.

Gaia, to her surprise, did not want to leave. She had slept here, with little consequence. She had eaten and lived well.

"If ever you come to Korthos, Malechon and Hora," she told them, on the pier, "you may stay as long as you like."

Hora placed one of her feathered charms in Gaia's hands. "Hang this in your bedroom," she said, "and the nightmares will cease."

And so they boarded the ship, and left. Korthos—their home—awaited.

THEMURIA

"Here there are titans," Theron's old friend Zoë had told him, on the first trip to Themuria.

It seemed a lifetime ago. Years had gone by, and he himself had changed. He missed the days when he hadn't been hunted, when he didn't have all these pressures weighing him down. But the companionship of Aigon had made things better. He had a great challenge ahead of him; but it was a challenge he'd never have to face alone.

As they made their way up the mountainous terrain, through lakes and streams, Zoë's warning was close to his heart. He faced a greater threat than titans now, but how quickly they could end him. The Oracle had foresight and knowledge, and her Maids had their daggers, but Titans wielded hammers of thunder and lightning.

"Here there are titans," Theron said aloud as he climbed up a mountainous stretch of land. Aigon traversed the difficult terrain with ease, but the strenuous exercise had begun to wear on Theron. His legs and arms were sore from these days of journeying. He wondered if they should have taken the road openly, with all its risks.

"Titans," Aigon said, "the Sons of Chaos. They are a vestige, a remnant, of when the gods walked the earth… As long as we respect them and keep away from them, they won't harm us."

And yet Theron had boldly challenged a titan, against his better judgment. He would not make that mistake again. He was not strong enough, not yet.

As they continued to push through the rough terrain, the event of last week haunted him. That creature, part serpentine, part humanoid, was etched into his memory. The more he thought about it, the more he believed it was some pet or beast-of-burden the Oracle used to sniff out their prey, like a huntsman's hound. If there was one of them, there were surely more.

Late in the day, when Theron wasn't sure he could go on, when the climb was causing him serious pain, right as he was about to give up, they reached the crest of a mountain and saw, below them, surrounded by pines, the village of Arkadion. From here, it was all downhill, an easy walk, as long as they didn't fall in a crevasse or stumble. Yet Aigon was hesitant.

More than ever, he was showing signs of his trepidation.

"If Phillipidēs couldn't defeat the Oracle," Aigon probably thought, "then surely Theron can't."

And yet, over these days, Theron had become more determined than ever. Betrayal was the ultimate sin; and the Oracle had betrayed him. He had trusted her, and then she sent her Maids to slay him. Just like she had done to Phillipidēs, lying to him to ensure his death, the Oracle had betrayed Theron as well.

And Theron remained mystified, as well, that the Oracle thought he had the gift of prophecy. Where had she gotten that notion? Had she imagined it? Was jealousy the root of her hate? Had she also made the same mistake about Phillipidēs, and therefore focused on him with burning hatred? It seemed possible.

Though Arkadion was close, the sun set while they were descending through the forest.

They stopped by the waters of a cold lake.

Did the Oracle know how close they were? Surely she had an idea. The body of the serpent creature, her tracking hound, had given them away. So what now? What more did she have up her sleeve? They had to be more cautious than ever. They had to watch out for any sign of their pursuers. Who knew how close they were?

As dusk settled in, Theron disrobed and waded into the water with a net, intending to go fishing. As he searched, he listened intently to all the noises around him, the songbirds, the occasional crunching of a twig, the squirrels shimmying up the trees. He had to remain cautious.

He returned to camp that night, to the raging fire which Aigon had started, with a net of three trout, still squirming. It was among his best attempts to fish to date.

When they devoured the fish later that night, some of Theron's strength began to return. He felt, for this first time in a long while, that he could fight the Maids of Prophecy, and win. Even with all their dark powers, he had a chance of defeating them. Or so he thought.

Yet as Aigon ate, there was a pained look on his face. He had the look of a man, certain he was headed to his doom. Theron's determination didn't ease his concerns. Just a week ago, his pleas to turn back had been frequent; only now did he fully accept what Theron wanted. Aigon, the hero's tutor, would follow him, even to certain death. Aigon had Theron's thanks and gratitude.

"Are you ready?" Aigon said to him that night. "Are you ready, for the end of your world?"

BOS, THENOA-KERSICA BORDER

The fortress watched over the bridge to Kersica, as it had for centuries.

In better times, the way had been open, allowing traders from Eloesus to bring their wares inland. Now, locked in mutual distrust and hostility, no one was allowed pass Bos, on either side, and armies faced each other in a tenuous peace.

When Khloë arrived with battalion after battalion, a war horn blew. They had caught them by surprise. But almost instantly the battle began.

Khloë, in the manner of amazon generals, fought at the front lines with her sabers. The Kersican soldiers, in their red capes and form-fitting breastplates, were better armed and armored. But the speed of the assault, the quickness of the charge, caught them off guard.

Khloë, with her sabers, struck three dead and—as the army pressed the Kersicans—it was a matter of hours before they broke ranks.

They had been trained to never retreat, on pain of death; but the suddenness of the assault had broken them.

And open war had been declared once more, open war between the Kersican League and the Thenoans. The die had been cast; and either destruction or total victory would ensue. Khloë would do her best to ensure the latter.

Night settled in and the country beyond Bos was silent. Khloë marched, at the head of the Free and Democratic Army of Thénai, behind enemy lines.

Whatever happened, whatever storm took her… it had been the decision of herself and Chairon to do this. She would not rest until victory was assured.

KORTHOS HARBOR

The journey home had been uneventful, and though—with the charm hanging above her sleeping quarters—no nightmares had assailed her, Gaia remained unsettled, and a dark cloud hung over her. The fear of Nix had driven away the fear of the demiurge. But how long would it last? How long before the charm's effects wore thin?

The ship had just pulled into the harbor, and though the sight of land was welcome, there was no relief in Gaia's heart.

She had secluded herself in all this time, keeping away even from Korë and her trusted servants. She had left her private quarters on the ship only rarely; for dinner or for bodily functions. Although Nix of the Silvered Sword had purged her nightmares, was she not worse off? Still, she lived her life on edge, afraid of shadows, afraid of the night. No feathered charm could take that away.

~

There was a foreignness to these streets. She had been gone a long time, and she had changed over these months, for the worse, but beyond the Long Walls, amid the deteriorating streets and crumbling buildings, she did sense a real shift.

Everyone seemed to be keeping an eye out for themselves. There were fewer smiles and no laughs. Had the war with Thénai fallen into a downward trajectory?

With the death of the Dark Captain, was there a growing realization that, even with the aid of the Kersicans, they had no chance?

Would the Kings of Kersepoli agree to a truce, a de facto surrender? Gaia had her doubts, but maybe it was possible. Would enough bloodshed, enough misspent wealth and treasure, cause them to abandon this foolish war once and for all?

She was getting ahead of herself.

And she was ill.

She hurried home as fast as she could, and her servants struggled to keep up, hauling cases of luggage through the crowded thoroughfares.

HOUSE OF THE SATYR, KORTHOS

The walls were bright and newly whitewashed. The picture frames had been dusted and polished; the silvers, displayed in the entryway, gleamed in the window's light.

Home… there was no place like it, though Gaia loved being under the care of Hora and her patron goddess.

The quiet halls and corridors, the cheery hearth, it all comforted her. Though home had its share of darkness and sad memories, she was glad to be here.

~

Gaia's husband was sitting outside, on the portico. Normally they would go weeks without speaking. But she had gotten back from a long trip. Surely Arkedamon would care to see her, even briefly, just to say hello.

It was a lonely world. Without Rogon to share it, Gaia had begun to feel hollow.

Did the fear of becoming a widow start all this? Did it cause her hallucinations of the demiurge?

Had she—now separated from Rogon, stung by the bitter pill of rejection and then widowhood—dreamed up this haunting? Was it all the effect of an embittered mind, of a grieving soul?

No. The nightmares were too real. They stretched from the realm of dreams into the real world. She felt the demiurge's haunting presence everywhere.

Out in the portico, the wind was blowing, providing a respite against the day's heat. The noise and foul smells of the city were evident here, but Arkedamon sat unbothered, enjoying a glass of wine as he looked down onto the streets below.

As she had expected, but not as she had hoped, Arkedamon didn't look to her or acknowledge her presence. According to city records, and the Book of Ceremonies in the temple, Arkedamon and Gaia were wed. They shared a home.

But other than that, they were strangers.

Sometimes she wept for those days. She had married Arkedamon with some semblance of hope that this political arrangement would blossom into love; she'd been disappointed. In the Temple to Arephon, they had pledged their vows and signed their names in the Book.

Beyond the portico, in the High City more than a mile away, the still-ruined temple could be seen.

Reconstruction had begun, but money had dwindled amid the turmoil of war. Would the Temple of Arephon ever stand proudly again, as it had when Gaia and Arkedamon were wed?

"It has been a while," Gaia said.

To her surprise, Arkedamon turned to face her.

"You look terrible."

Gaia laughed at his brusqueness. Arkedamon smiled. Was this the warmest moment they'd had in years? The iciness of his stare was gone for a moment, but it quickly returned. There was no love between them.

As both Gaia and Arkedamon's political ambitions faltered, what did they have in common? What reason did they have to share their lives? It seemed all that bound them together was this House, the House of the Satyr, where they'd spent these decades. It was a flimsy glue to bind two people who hated each other.

"But yes," Arkedamon said. "It's been a while."

Gaia wondered how much he knew of her situation. The walls of the House of the Satyr were thin. It was not difficult to eavesdrop.

The Gauntlet, stowed away in the lockbox, had struggled to break free. Had Arkedamon heard its rattling? What did he think of her haunting? Could he hear her screams, her tossing and turning, her terror in the night? Did he care? Of course not. But perhaps he knew. Perhaps he knew what ailed Gaia. Perhaps the demiurge had touched him as well.

At last the servants caught up with her, noisily ascending the staircase. Korë had brought with her bushels of pomegranates and figs from the market. Malchos was heaving one of her luggage cases. It was Vidros, approaching her with the feathered charm, that took her aback.

The wreath of feathers, with two crossed daggers and a skull in the center, had stopped her nightmares. But what would Arkedamon think of her using it?

"Where should I put this, Your Worship?" said Vidros.

Gaia smiled. Her face flushed hot in embarrassment. Arkedamon was a rationalist. He would not understand; and then he'd tell all of his friends in the House of Assembly.

"Toss it out," she said. "Throw it away."

Instantly she regretted her words; she regretted her command.

But Arkedamon was looking at her with a new respect. "You surprise me sometimes, Gaia," he said. "I'm glad you're back."

~

Summer, in Korthos, was a dreadful affair. Those with money retreated to homes in the outlying hills. Others, like Gaia, who were secluded and had little recourse, tried their best to stay out of the sunlight, and to remain still. Wealthy men, and demiarchs, could have their dinner parties in the country. As for

Gaia, the House of the Satyr would remain her home, her prison.

In her absence, her house servants had kept her bedroom clean. Her bedsheets were tucked neatly along the mattress. The curtains had been cleaned, no doubt washed and dried, and not a speck of mold or dust could be seen on the walls.

Many in Korthos would believe she led a charmed life. But would the shoemakers and the carpenters, the coppersmiths and the tinsmiths, the hostlers and the fletchers think so if they experienced a moment of her pain? They spent their lives in toil, much of it thankless. But had they ever been visited by a creature from beyond? Had the red eyes of the demiurge ever looked upon them? Would they take a life of wealth and comfort, if they also dreaded sundown like she did?

She caught Vidros downstairs. He was scrubbing the floors of the kitchen with a sponge. Suds lay heavy over the wooden floors. She was afraid to ask what was on her mind.

"Vidros," she said. "Where did you put the charm?"

"I threw it away, like you asked."

Gaia's stomach twisted to knots. She had brought this on herself. She could blame no one else.

"A shame," she said.

The sun set, and from her closet the demiurge emerged.

He stroked his ice cold hand against her cheek. "Thou tried to escape me," he purred. "But I have marked you for my own."

~

A bell rang, in a timbre and melody she recognized as the

House of the Archon, calling demiarchs to business.

Though Gaia's star had fallen considerably, she was privy to these events, and welcomed there.

Rattled by last night, she needed a distraction. As she looked in the mirror with cosmetics in hand, she saw she had regressed to her state weeks ago. Her cheeks were sunken; her face was pale. She was skeletal.

She wept as she donned her robe of gold cloth. No amount of powder and Ink-of-Tyrhenos could hide her deterioration. She was a ghost. She was not herself. She feared she would die soon.

~

Korthians on the street gawked at her as she walked by. She should have worn a hood and veil.

It has truly gotten this bad.

Flanked by her servants, she still drew attention. She cursed the gods, and fate, for her lot. Once known for her beauty, now Korthos regarded her as a ghoul.

Would she hole up in the House of the Satyr, and never leave again? Perhaps that was best.

~

In the House of Assembly, two-hundred demiarchs had gathered, and the archon was seated on the dais.

Gaia had been gone for months. She sensed a change.

There was tension in the room, tension beyond what she'd experienced in the recent past. What had shifted? What was new? Had the Thenoans finally broken the stalemate? Was slaughter in their future? They had fought this war a long time… would they lose?

The demiarchs began speaking. "King Helion has moved against us," said one. "We must act…"

"Don't call him king… don't give him that respect." The demiarch's voice was small, petty, bitter.

"We are at war with the Kersicans?" cried Gaia. Silence ensued in the House of Assembly. With Korthos severely in debt, with a badly-stretched army, how could they possibly hold off against the Thenoans?

"A divided nation falls!" she cried, quoting Ansolon. "A nation warring with itself will crumble!"

Had she truly come home to this grave crisis? It was a crisis they could not recover from. It had to be solved.

The demiarchs were growling at her. "You've been gone all this time, Gaia!" sneered a demiarch she recognized as Gorgios. "What do you know?"

"And what have they done, so grievously, that you would ruin the war effort and collapse our alliance?" She was shouting. Perhaps it was the stress of her nightmares wearing on her. Perhaps she'd just had enough.

The demiarchs were glaring at her.

"Tell that to our farmers," said Gorgios, "gouged for prices… forced to receive a pittance at the edge of the sword."

A grain dispute… surely they weren't that short-sighted. What was the suffering of farmers compared to the destruction of the Kersican League, and Thenoan victory?

The archon Phaistion stood there on his golden seat. Gaia had built a relationship with him; she had earned his trust. Surely he saw this madness. "Phaistion… you will throw out the war effort over a price dispute?"

"The Kersicans are vile savages and uncultured…" Phaistion's face turned a cherry red. "They seize the wealth of others by violence!"

Perhaps Gaia had been naïve all along, to think that Kersepoli and Korthos could ever forge a lasting alliance. Could any of the cities in Eloesus, with their history of enmity and war, ever agree to work together? The task was too massive, the list of grievances unforgettable.

"Remember Bactris!" shouted a demiarch whose name she did not know.

Bactris, once a city in Korthos, had been seized by the Kersicans. She, of course, remembered. Even when they joined together as a league, the kings of Kersepoli refused to hand it back. Yet Korthos had swallowed its pride; and given its blessing to this unlikely alliance.

Why now?

Gaia thought she knew. Together, the city put on a brave face, a united front. But tensions existed from the beginning, and this ham-handed attempt at extortion by the Kersicans had caused open warfare to result.

Gaia, still frail from her long months of suffering, still felt a deep obligation to Korthos and its people. If she looked deep within herself, perhaps she'd find the strength she needed to solve this problem, to allow reason to prevail, to ensure that the unlikely alliance was maintained. But she had thrown away the one thing that protected her from her nightmares, the charm which Hora had given her.

The House of Assembly had devolved into a shouting match. Gaia feared they were on the edge of a brawl.

"Enough!" Gaia cried, and to her surprise the hall became silent. "I will go. I will speak to the Kings of Kersepoli. I will hear them out, and I will give them our demands. I will make peace."

She expected laughter. More scoffing. More looks of contempt and derision.

Instead, Phaistion said, "There is no better person for the

task, man or woman."

She had served as an ambassador before; now she'd serve as one again, to her supposed allies.

~

Before she embarked on her journey, she traveled to Heaven's Square, and—amid the towering marble temples—turned off onto a main thoroughfare, then another street, then another dark alley.

Before she left the Isle of Salitis, Hora had told her more about her religion and deep faith.

Sitting by the seashore, Hora had said, "The Cult of Nix as you know it is a false one. The true Cult of Nix, which saves the troubled, is harder to find."

Hora had given her explicit instructions where to find the true temple, the temple which the goddess actually approved of. The true Temple of Nix, Hora said, was in Rat Alley, beyond a hidden door you could scarcely see.

Hora—one of the initiates—had given her the key.

The mudbrick walls that marked the alley were colored with dark stains. The roofs above blocked out most light. For all intents and purposes, it was night.

A rat scurried by her slipper and Gaia screamed. She thought Rat Alley was just a name, but she was wrong. When she continued her walk, she stepped carefully. She knew the scurrying shapes beside her could bite.

~

In the middle of the alley, where sunlight was negligible, Gaia—after much searching—found the door.

In the darkness, it blended in with the mudbrick walls. It

had the exact same color, and only someone searching would find it. She fit the key to the lock, and when it clicked, loosening the door with a groan, Gaia panicked and almost ran. But she steadied herself, took a deep breath, and remained calm.

She peered inside, and there, in the pitch darkness, she saw this was not a temple but an alcove.

She could not step inside. The space was too small.

And a skeleton stood there.

Gaia froze up.

Its form was mostly relegated to shadow. Its head, ribs, and arms, could just barely be seen.

It was dressed in rags, and its skull was glued with false hair. Eyes, fashioned from ivory, lay in its sockets.

Around the skeleton's neck was a feathered wreath, like the one Hora had given her.

The podium which the skeleton stood upon was etched in Old Eloesian:

SEEK THOU THE SECRETS OF THE WORLD.

Gaia took the wreath from her neck, careful not to touch bone. "I bid you goodbye, mother," she whispered to her. She shut the door and locked it.

OUTSIDE OF ARKADION, THEMURIA

On the coasts, Arkadians were a source of laughter. They were considered uncultured rustics, without knowledge of anything beyond their mountainous home.

To some extent, Theron knew, it was true. Most Arkadians never left. Some spent their entire lives within a mile of where they were born.

Yet many had left their sheltered life in the mountains and sought fortune in the coastal cities; they had made names for themselves and earned honors and praise.

They were good people; ignorant, perhaps, but good.

With Aigon hiding in the woods, fearful of drawing attention, Theron stood in plain view on the road. The wood and stone buildings of Arkadion lay before him, with the omnipresent Mount of Prophecy in the background. It was here that Theron would declare war.

If you want me, come and get me.

As he approached the town, the villagers stopped and gawked. There were no Maids of Prophecy in sight. There were no reptilian creatures, no Yawning Nymphs. To his surprise, the Arkadians stared at him for a while and then went about their daily chores.

If the appearance of a man in a lion's skin didn't faze them, what would?

The streets of Arkadion were unpaved, composed of dirt—

a sure sign of the village's poverty. The temple in the village square was carved of wood, and did not honor any of Eloesus' traditional gods but instead Brecko, lord of wine and frolic.

Its columns were plain, carved from cedars; it looked much like a coastland temple, with its pediment and red-tile roof, but not a bit of it was marble. The friezes running along its sides were also carved from wood but painted in bright colors, depending fat-bellied Brecko with his panther-skin, running from satyrs.

It was a hard life these Themurians lived, but they found a way to thrive. It was lonely, here, on the roof of the world.

Stormclouds were rolling in. A drizzle began to fall. There was thunder and lightning.

Theron needed a rest.

An inn lay on the edge of town, near the road. It was large and wooden, with a thatch roof, carved of logs. Smoke was billowing out from its chimney.

Up here, in the mountains, summer nights were colder than winter back on the coast.

He wondered if he should have told Aigon his plans.

But the centaur was patient. He would understand.

In his purchased room, he unslung his lion's skin from his head. His hair had grown wild and matted, greasy from all these months of hiking. As he stood there he knew hot water was being prepared. After all this time, he had some hope of rest.

He ate a meal of wild duck, with a deep goblet full of red wine. It was, by far, the best meal he'd had in months, and one which filled his stomach completely, and soothed his soul.

He could tell by the other patrons' reaction that his disheveled appearance and likely odor was unwelcome. That would change soon.

Outside, in the fenced-in courtyard, a tub full of steaming hot water had been prepared. A bath attendant handed Theron a chunk of lye soap.

When he stepped in the water, he almost recoiled at the heat. But he drew deeper in, and the weariness of the road began to fade. The cleansing power of the hot water overwhelmed him. He scrubbed with the lye soap, washing himself clean but also unwinding the knots in his body, the aches and pains caused by stress and fear, the long scars he bore from his months-long journey.

He emerged from the bath, an hour later, refreshed beyond his greatest dreams. His stomach was full. His mind was clear. His focus was keen.

So, too, did the reality of his situation dawn on him. He was unsafe here in *The Pot of Silver*. He was likely already compromised.

But the mattress of his bed was soft and stuffed with feathers. The sheets and blanket were clean: washed and dried in the sweet mountain air. When faced with such luxury, how could he resist.

He had already consented to the innkeeper's badgering— his clothes had been washed and hung out to dry. He couldn't leave now. Wrapped in a cloth, wearing only his underclothes, he ascended the stairs to his private room. A candle was burning on his bedside table. Nearby was a bowl of candied apples and a bottle of wine.

In Thénai's inns, such hospitality was unheard of.

Here, far from civilization, on the roof of the world, there was little culture and not much to do besides enjoy the lakes and streams. But the Arkadians were kind, and treated guests like family.

When Theron laid down on the bed and pulled the blankets over him, he fell asleep within moments.

The door burst open. Theron woke with a start and grabbed *Titan's Fist*. He swung before he saw the assailant, and crushed his skull.

No, *her*. A Maid of Prophecy lay dead and bleeding on the wood floor.

Loud shouts and screams echoed from the inn's main hall.

Amid the chaos, the moon was shining in through Theron's window.

He took no comfort in its light or the chirping of crickets outside. He rushed through the broken door, down into the hall, and saw tables overturned, chairs broken, and Aigon—whose head reached the ceiling—cutting down a Maid of Prophecy with his saber.

"You idiot!" Aigon was screaming. "What were you thinking staying here?"

There was blood on the wooden floor and blood on the walls. The windows had been smashed to smithereens; broken bottles of wine were shattered everywhere. And no doubt, the Oracle was sending more of her troops.

Theron rushed outside and grabbed his clothes which hung—now perfectly dried—on the line. He dressed quickly and again slung the lion's skin over his head. With *Titan's Fist* in hand, he rushed back inside and hopped on Aigon's back.

Aigon took off at a gallop.

"To the Mount of Prophecy!" Theron shouted. He shook

Titan's Fist and said, "I'll deliver this message straight to her."

KERSICA

The burning plains of Kersica were sapping Khloë's strength. Water was virtually impossible to find.

Back home, in Tigris, one only had to dig a few feet to find water, but here the earth was parched. The grass was yellow and wilting.

The troops had grown restless. But in the distance was the city she sought to take. The stone walls of Phalkis lay like a gray smudge in the horizon. But they were approaching.

The chains of the Elehoi would break. Liberty would return to Phalkis, liberty that was stolen who knew how long ago.

In the treaty which the Thenoan League had signed, all cities pledged to never stop fighting until every Elehoi breathed free, until every city in Kersica was liberated, until democracy—as Ansolon saw it—was the norm throughout all of Eloesus. That was what the Free and Democratic Armies pledged to do; that was what Khloë did even now.

Hours later, as the midday heat began to abate, they at last reached the stone walls of Phalkis. Khloë led the charge. Hoplites guarding the Elehoi rushed to fight, but they were outnumbered.

The Free and Democratic Army rushed over them like a wave.

An archer on the wall blew a horn.

Near Khloë, an Elehoi had been stamping grapes in a winepress.

Khloë watched as a Free and Democratic soldier sawed off the metal chains that bound his hands.

They were setting the Elehoi free. Liberty would return, just as they'd promised.

As the chains fell from his hands, the Elehoi was confused. He looked around, bewildered, in silence.

What do I do now, he was thinking. He had lived his life in servitude. He knew nothing other than labor and obeisance to his Kersican lord.

As the horns sounded, more Elehoi were—bit by bit—freed from their chains. But many more ran, no doubt afraid of the consequences. Living freely was alien to their minds. To them their masters were omnipresent and omnipotent; if they dared acquiesce to freedom, they'd be punished.

Like a wave the army descended on Phalkis. They swept around the city walls, cutting down red-caped hoplites who—to their credit—refused to flee, fighting to the death. Arrows pelted down from the battlements but the Free and Democratic Army surrounded the walls within minutes.

The horn of warning blew again, louder than ever.

They had cut off all contact with the outside world, all shipments of food and grain. The city would submit to liberation, as long as it might take.

Angelos, one of her Strategoi, approached Khloë as night began to set in. "The Elehoi…" he began. "What should we do with them?"

They stood behind him, a dozen of them, pitiful, naked. They wore nothing but loins. The women were bare breasted. Each of them was darkened by the sun, the product of hours of labor outside. Their hands were callused. They were gaunt and emaciated. And their bonds were broken; but their cufflinks remained, with the remnants of chains still dangling from them.

"Elehoi," Khloë said. She remembered who these people were: once free citizens of Phalkis, they had been sold into bondage and brutalized. "Let them go," she said. "Set them free."

Angelos looked uncertain.

"Let them go," Khloë repeated. It was an order.

Wordlessly, the Elehoi ran. The road was long. She feared they would perish. But they'd taste freedom before they died.

A weeping dove was singing as the sun rose. Its song, like a dirge, filled the morning with its gloom.

The fighting had died down. The city, surrounded, was surely thinking of its terms for surrender.

The gates opened. A horn blew. Out from the city of Phalkis came a rider on a white horse. His cape and the horsehair crest of his helmet were a bright crimson. He wore a bronze breastplate forged in the shape of muscles and carried a spear in his hand. This was a Stratego, or someone of great importance.

According to the law of warfare, the Free and Democratic Army remained still, refusing to storm the city gate. One never harmed a messenger, or impaired a negotiation.

He came galloping out of Phalkis and reared up on his horse, pulling the rains.

"Thenoans." He spoke the word like it was a curse. "I will speak to your leader."

When he realized their leader was Khloë, he gawked.

"An amazon!" he scoffed.

Was the sight impossible? An amazon, leading an Eloesian army?

Surely, it had seemed impossible to Khloë until very recently. But she was a Thenoan. She had pledged her allegiance to the people of Thénai; she had brought an offering before the civic gods. She was one of them. Her name was in the register of citizens. She was a Thenoan, not an amazon, and she always would be.

"She is our amazon," shouted Angelos.

The hoplites around her raised their spears and cheered.

The derision did not leave the Kersicans face; instead it deepened. He narrowed his eyes as he surveyed the Free and Democratic Army. "The City of Phalkis offers terms of surrender," he said. "We will all vacate this city, everyone. You may take a hundred pounds in gold…"

"We didn't come here for gold!" said Khloë. "We came here to fight. And we will fight until all of your Elehoi are free."

The Kersican sneered. "We will butcher our Elehoi before you lay hands on them," he said. "An Elehoi cannot know freedom. They are animals. They are mules."

As he rode back into Phalkis and the gates rolled shut, Khloë thought about what she had seen. In a city like Phalkis, it was likely that only a hundred civilians were full-blooded male citizens, and the rest were women or Elehoi. Women, like Elehoi, were not viewed as having full rights in Kersica. In a world that valued war, only male power was valued. The hearth and home, the arts, the beauty of nature, were all scorned.

As the sun set, Khloë walked up to Angelos. "Gather wood. We lay siege soon."

GATE OF STORMS, KORTHOS

A grain dispute!

Gaia laughed at the thought as her carriage rattled down the road.

Had they truly thrown away the war effort because of a grain dispute?

"They are robbers," the archon Phaistion had told her, quaking with rage. "They have always been robbers, the Kersicans."

The farmers could not survive on those prices, he had said. The farmers who supported the hoplites and the war effort were being crushed—all at the edge of the sword, at the threat of violence by their Kersican oppressors.

Gaia did not know if she could talk sense into these people.

But it was a welcome distraction. For days, the threat of nightmares had been the last thing on her mind.

And yet, as she left the safe harbor of home, she knew night was coming. She stood up as the carriage rattled back and forth. She hung her charm up on the carriage ceiling. She said a prayer, "Save me, mother," though she was still not entirely sure that she believed.

Fear of Nix overcame fear of all else. For that, Gaia had She of the Silvered Sword to thank.

The charm looked much like the one she'd thrown away. The feathers around the wreath were dyed in bright pinks and blacks. A ceramic skull of fired clay lay in its center. Two daggers of silver held the wreath together.

There was so much symbolism contained within, so much she did not understand about the faith. Would Hora be able to explain? Could she tell her about the "Silvered Sword" Nix held, about the "Seven Gates" she had opened, about the "Silver Stair" which she stood upon?

Gaia did not know any of it. But she did know that when the charm hung over her, the nightmares ceased. The cold, dread presence of Nix overshadowed the terror of the demiurge.

The Lady of the Night was not without her terror, of course. But under her patronage, Gaia felt protected.

Did she believe? Her father and her family would laugh at the things she believed now. They would scoff at the charm she hung above her bed, if they were alive. To acknowledge the gods was to be welcomed in public life; to have faith was to be scorned and exiled.

After all, Gaia had thought Hora insane when she'd first met her. Now Gaia thought Hora was the wisest woman she'd ever known.

She opened the shutters of the carriage facing home. The Gate of Storms was drawing further away. Its lintel, etched in thunderbolts painted bright blue, symbols of the storm god, reminded her of the familiar haunt she was leaving. It was not without its troubles and fears, but could she afford to leave the comfort of home? The charm which hung in her carriage had not completely banish the demiurge's presence. Still, Gaia dreaded sundown.

On the shelf beside her carriage bed, there was a gold backed mirror. She looked at herself in the reflection, seeing she had not improved much in these past days. Fear was written over her, and the weight of many months of suffering. She had hoped her return home would soothe her soul; but she was still deteriorating, still losing weight, still growing weak. Her appetite had not increased.

Was the patronage of Nix worth nothing?

She had brought bread and several bottles of wine for the first leg of her journey. Wine she could sip, in small intervals. But even late in the day, she'd prefer to go hungry. Once she had loved life in all its energy, in all its triumphs and travails, in all her schemes to climb Korthos' halls of power. Now she counted her days, and wondered when her life would be snuffed out—when the black hand of the demiurge would reach out from beyond and take her. How long before she joined her mother and father among the dead? She had one foot in the grave, one foot in the world of the living.

She looked out onto the tombs beside the road. Would she join them soon? How soon? Was it days, or hours?

~

The moon was full, shining bright amid the stars. Wisps of gray cloud obscured some like a cloak, but it had not rained in weeks. In ancient days, travelers along the Sun King's Road had to fear lions. Now Gaia only listened for the howling of wolves. Mostly they stayed away from humans, but Gaia still worried about them, like she had been worrying about everything.

Her servants had left her in utter solitude. They could provide protection against physical threats: bandits, panthers and yes, wolves. But within the carriage Gaia fought a greater foe, a foe she could not shake in all these months.

She had opened a portal to the demiurge's world. Was it her fault that he had taken her captive.

She had eaten nothing all day. She still had no appetite. From the shelf she took a bottle of wine, and poured herself a glass. In the cramped carriage it was difficult to sleep, even with the vehicle stopped and a feather bed set out. She took a few sips but even the wine was unsettling to her. She set it aside.

The summer night was as hot as any she remembered, but she went to bed covered in goosebumps. Her hand was trembling. Was it the demiurge she feared, or Nix?

"Banish my terror, O mother," Gaia whispered.

Hours later, she drifted to sleep.

She dreamed that night that she stood in Thénai's City Square. The sun was alone amid a blue sky.

People went about their daily tasks. But the earth was quaking. And up above, in the firmament, there were signs of the end.

Rogon blotted out the sky: her former lover, clad in armor, eyes burning like bonfires of the night. He was cloaked in clouds, as large as a god, and yet the citizens of Thénai did not notice him. Only Gaia could see him as he grew larger and larger, until he was the size of the earth itself. His body darkened to shadow, until he was featureless. He had become the demiurge.

Fire and earthquakes ensued; the High City collapsed and the temple with it. Troubles continued until the end, until the seas boiled with sulfur and the sky turned black with ash.

At the end of the world, when the mountains were rent, Gaia and the demiurge stood alone, hands clasped, he her husband and she his wife.

OUTSIDE MOUNT HYLEA, THEMURIA

Thunder and lightning, pelting rain and whipping wind greeted Theron as he rode up the mountain on Aigon's back. It was as if the Oracle sent this weather to halt them in their tracks. It would not work.

Theron and Aigon barreled ahead up the path.

In Theron's absence things had changed. Structures had been built along the road: colonnades built of white marble and columns shaped like Maids of Prophecy; torches which refused to wink out despite the pouring rain and statues of prancing satyrs. The Oracle had grown in wealth and she had grown in power. Her influence now extended throughout all of Eloesus.

In Theron's lifetime her temple had sat empty. He had played an unfortunate part in her resurgence and rebirth. Now the Ruined Temple had its priestess. The Oracle was alive and well, and she was out for Theron's blood.

If Theron had caused this catastrophe, it was his responsibility to end it.

The road was narrow and slick with mud as it wound its way past steep rock faces and precarious slopes. Aigon, ever sure-footed, never missed a step, but Theron was convinced a horse would slip and fall. These conditions were brutal, even though they faced no Maids of Prophecy or servants of the Oracle. The storm threatened to take them all down in a mudslide.

Perhaps the storm was also the Oracle's doing.

It would not prevent Theron from his mission. There was too much rage within him, built up over these weeks and years.

Titan's Fist thirsted for blood.

Late in the night—he could hardly see it—but rocks came tumbling down in a landslide, blocking the way.

"She is afraid!" Theron shouted.

"No," Aigon said, "the Oracle fears nothing."

Theron was sure of it. Why else had she commanded this storm to arrive, except to block his path? She knew he could overcome her. She knew he could destroy her and throw her temple to ruin. That is why she feared her, why she sought to prevent her from coming.

Out of the noise of pelting rain and booming thunder, the sound of a drum-beat distinguished itself. Below them, past several switchbacks, the light of torches shone in the darkness. A procession was following them, a procession of the Oracle's servants.

The wall of rocks was insurmountable, at least for now. The more Aigon tried to scramble over it, the more his hooves sunk into the mud and pebbles. Theron hopped off Aigon's back and batted *Titan's Fist*. If they wanted a fight, they would get one. Theron would never back down.

He waited, and Aigon waited with him, bow in hand. The drums grew louder as the procession ascended the road, up its numerous switchbacks. In the whipping wind and rain, they marched in unison, calmly, slowly. At their front, two Maids of Prophecy bore torches. One, an older woman, held a sword in her hand.

Panic was welling up inside Theron. He bit his lip and tried to remain calm. He could not overreact; he couldn't let his emotions get the best of him.

But memories stuck to him, dreadful memories of the

Yawning Nymph whose pain he still remembered, whose scars he still bore.

Was this mission stupid? Was it ill-conceived from the beginning?

Amara, he prayed, *you gave Phillipidēs your sword and shield, and the Mirror of Truth. Will you protect me as well?*

What had happened to him? He had come here so boldly. Now his stomach had turned to jelly. Where was the bravery and anger he'd felt just moments before?

The drumbeat continued and though the rain poured and the wind blew, the Maids of Prophecy did not moderate their slow march. Up they walked, slowly, steadily, up the switchbacks and the winding mountain road.

Aigon scrambled ahead, perhaps seeking some route of escape but seeing none. He turned to Theron, a half-panicked look in his eye, and said, "Get ready."

Get ready for death were his unspoken words, communicated by the terror on his face.

As the Maids of Prophecy turned up the switchback facing them, Aigon let loose a volley of arrows. None reached their target. The Maids of Prophecy dodged artfully, seeming to know when each arrow would hit and where.

Aigon dropped his bow and scrambled backward. A hoof slipped under pebbles and he almost careened over the ledge. He drew his saber.

Theron wondered if this ill-advised quest would cost Aigon his life.

He had chosen this risky path for himself, but he couldn't bear the thought of costing the life of another.

As the procession of Maids continued, Theron batted back *Titan's Fist* and charged headlong into their ranks.

He swung wildly but each blow was countered; every strike

was dodged or driven back. The more Theron attacked, the more they dodged. Soon they had encircled him.

Aigon came galloping ahead.

The woman with the sword stepped up.

"Stop!" Theron shouted and Aigon reared up on his hind legs, even as the sword came whistling within an inch of his throat.

Pandemonium broke loose; screams of anger and wild, savage blows. The Maids of Prophecy unveiled their hidden daggers. In the chaos, Theron's blows began to land. Soon he had crushed skulls; bodies slid down the mountain road, and blood flowed like a river.

In a panicked moment, all of Theron's foes had fallen dead.

"It seems," he said absently, "this wasn't supposed to happen." He did not know what he meant.

"No," Aigon said. "This was not supposed to happen."

In the darkness of the night, the blood that dripped off his saber was inky black.

Together Aigon and Theron climbed over the mound of stones. Within an hour, they had crossed the barrier.

The Lonely Temple, and justice, awaited.

PHALKIS, KERSICA

The ballistas, the war towers, the battering rams had been carved of wood. The engineers of the Free and Democratic Army were finishing them with nails and screws. The hour of the siege approached.

And a horn blew.

When Khloë looked to her left, panic consumed her.

A column formed, still barely visible. Soldiers in crimson capes and helmets approached. Their line was a hundred strong on its face. How many thousands had come to lift the siege?

And worse, she knew just what had caused it.

Those Elehoi they freed had turned on them.

Were they afraid of their Kersican masters? Did they fear escape more than they feared slavery?

The Free and Democratic Armies had, perhaps, been naïve to think breaking the chains of the Elehoi would turn them into allies.

But they would continue breaking those chains, despite the risks.

"We will not rest," their charter said, "until every chain is broken, until every Elehoi is set free…"

She could not panic in front of her troops. She had a sacred duty. She was their leader.

Marching to her orders, the hoplites of the Free and Democratic Armies joined, shield to shield, and stuck out their spears.

They would face the day and fight together.

The Kersicans fell upon them suddenly, as the night was darkening and the sun had begun to set below the horizon. The shield wall held, and hours later, after a long stalemate, the night had begun to set in, and they drew backward.

The night had saved him. The darkness had prevented disaster.

In the morning they fought again.

Hours before sunset, the Kersicans began to falter. Their shield wall cracked. Confusion began to set in and Khloë pressed the advance.

Like they'd been taught since birth, the Kersicans did not retreat. One by one they fell, together with their shields. There was not a single coward among them.

At dusk, when they counted their dead, some two-hundred young men were sent back to their families in Thénai. They had won the day; they had salvaged the siege. Those young men's sacrifice was not in vain; but how long could this campaign last? The Kersicans were alerted. Trouble was headed their way.

~

One week later, the gate gave in to the pressure of the battering ram.

Khloë charged into the city at the front of them all, slashing wildly with their sabers.

The Kersicans fought, as was their nature, to the bloody

end.

When the Kersicans sacked a city, they executed every adult male and turned the survivors into Elehoi.

No doubt many of Khloë's soldiers wanted to do the same to them.

"Show mercy!" she shouted as her soldiers stormed the streets and broke into homes.

"We shall never loot or rob from the cities we conquer," the Free and Democratic charter stated, but so much of the charter was unworkable and impossibly idealistic.

The City of Phalkis had its treasures, but like most cities of the Kersican plains, its dwellings were plain and threadbare. Luxury was unknown.

Hours after the city was taken, Orestion, one of the Strategoi, approached Khloë. "There are thousands of Elehoi in the city," he said. "Should we execute them?"

Logic demanded that they would. Especially after the Elehoi they freed had run away and told their superiors, the Free and Democratic Armies would have little patience for compassion.

Yet there were greater things, more important things, than a logical choice. "We will not rest until every chain is broken," Khloë repeated the words of the charter. "Until every Elehoi is set free…"

Orestion left her sight, taking the idle words as a command.

Within moments, the sounds of chains breaking echoed all around her. Against her better senses, against her own logic, they broke the binds of the Elehoi.

"One day," Khloë whispered to the wind, "you will all be

free."

The blue-and-gold laurel wreath flag of Thénai was planted on every turret of the wall. Phalkis had been claimed and liberated.

They controlled an empty city. Without its Elehoi, without its slaves, nothing remained except buildings.

Phalkis had no wealth. There were no works of gold or silver objects of art. If Phalkis ever had luxuries in its history, they were taken away to Kersepoli and melted into coin.

No beauty, no enjoyment, only hard labor and exercise…. That was the Kersican way.

For Khloë, it felt like home.

SUN KING'S ROAD, KORTHICA

Despite frequent stops, the carriage ride had become almost unbearable for Gaia.

Between the nightmares and the summer heat, she feared she had taken ill. A cough had started, a fever had consumed her, and stepping out for just a few moments caused dizziness. She had blocked the sun from the carriage windows. She had come to detest the light. In total darkness she sat, hoping any moment that one of her servants would shout "We've arrived!" And yet how could she conduct diplomacy in this state? How was it possible? She could scarcely walk or talk. She could hardly function.

The air in the carriage was stuffy. Perhaps it was causing her nausea. She lifted the shutters of the carriage and shouted, "Stop!"

When she stepped out, the sun was blinding in its intensity. In the hateful heat and brightness, she wanted to cower, but at least the air was clear and fresh, and she could breathe. On either side of the carriage, along the Sun King's Road, fields of golden wheat stretched into the distance. It was almost ripe for the cutting. She thought of stealing a few grains for herself, but quickly thought better of it.

Korë approached her. "Are you all right, Your Grace?"

"We are near Kersepoli, no?" said Gaia.

Korë's glum expression betrayed her answer. "We've stopped every few hours," she said.

The words stung Gaia. She was responsible for the slow pace. But this misery, inflicted by the demiurge, was not her fault.

How did she know when she activated the Gammahedron that the demiurge would see her from beyond the portal, and mark her as her own?

In the distance, a stream ran through the fields of wheat. The Sun King's Road continued via a bridge. Fresh, cold water might heal her.

In the streams of clear water, her warped reflection shimmered in the sun. In these days she had grown more gaunt. She had no appetite. She needed to find one, or else her life was in peril.

She removed her slippers and set her feet in the cold water.

Korë grabbed a brush from the folds of her blue robe and untied Gaia's hair, then began to brush it. "Are you up for this task, Your Grace?" Korë said. "Are you sure you can handle it? Should we go home?"

In her heart, Gaia wanted just that, to turn back and give up. But she couldn't accept failure after the House of Assembly had sent her. She had a civic duty, a patriotic duty.

The icy water soothed her, washing away the dirt and must as it meandered toward the sea, many miles away. A lizard sunning on the rock skittered away like a shadow.

"Your Grace," said Korë, "you haven't been yourself for months."

When she admitted to Korë everything that happened, she sounded like a madwoman. Perhaps she had just imagined all that had gone on before. Perhaps the Gauntlet was a figment of madness.

But Korë clasped her hand in Gaia's. "I'm sorry, Your

Grace," she said.

"Call me Gaia."

"Gaia," Korë said. "You should never have agreed to this."

"I know…"

Korë stood up and, having brushed Gaia's hair, began to work it into a braid. "Is that why you have that feather charm in the carriage?" she said. "To protect you from the dreams?"

Surely the charm was gossiped about among all of Gaia's servants.

"Philemon said it's a charm… it has something to do with the goddess Nix."

"He's right," Gaia muttered. "And it stopped working days ago. The nightmares returned. These nightmares will end me."

"Nix won't save you," said Korë. "She is as cruel and frightening as the demiurge…"

"Religion won't save me," Gaia corrected her. "The gods are frauds…"

Hushed silence ensued. Gaia forgot her company. Among many—and perhaps most—crowds, such words would be considered inexcusable and mark Gaia as a pariah. It did not matter if the words were true. It did not matter that Gaia's prayer and ritual failed to cure her. It only mattered that norms were respected, that the gods and goddesses were never defamed, that figments of imagination were honored and revered like they had been for centuries. Insulting those marble statues, those gold icons which Eloesus revered was somehow the greatest crime of all. Gaia didn't care. Nix had failed her. The gods had failed her.

For the sake of her health, she thought she should turn back now; but she couldn't face the House of Assembly in failure. She had to push on. She had to brave the terrors of the night. She had to reach Kersepoli and negotiate an agreement, or else the war was lost. That much was clear.

She splashed her feet in the water as Korë's artful hands finished up the braid.

"I should go back," Gaia repeated.

"Yes, you should," Korë said, "but you won't."

Korë knew Gaia well. Gaia was not one to give up on things, even at great pains to herself.

"You're right," Gaia whispered, "I won't."

That night, when the carriage stopped, there was an earthquake.

Bottles of wine shattered; Gaia, tripping out of the carriage, fell on her face. She wondered if the stars overhead would shake loose and drop like figs. In the silence that followed, she knew something had irrevocably changed. She grew ravenously hungry. She ate all the road bread that remained.

She slept well and woke up refreshed, without any nightmare or terror.

Word spread throughout the land: "Mount Kronos has erupted again!"

THE RUINED TEMPLE, MOUNT HYLEA

The night was dark, and clouds obscured the stars and moon.

Instead, lightning illumined the night: spears and forks of lightning, spitting and crackling. The rain in a downpour, blowing this way and that with the wind.

And Theron approached the Ruined Temple amid the gale, with *Titan's Fist* in hand, ready to slay the Oracle and stop her evil once and for all.

Lightning erupted just feet in front of Theron. Sparks spat and flew as it struck the stone pathway leading up to the Ruined Temple.

In the light that followed, Theron saw—in the distance— the Oracle slumped in her throne, her sightless white eyes glimmering, a scepter dangling idly in her hand. The snake wrapped around her leg and body slithered from under her and disappeared into the shadows.

She looked different than the last time Theron saw her. She seemed bigger, stronger, more vital.

The closer Theron grew, the more the gnawing in the pit of his stomach intensified. Not for the first time, he questioned the wisdom of his decision.

Satyrs darted away like shadows as he approached.

The Oracle stood up, leaning on her scepter. "Theron," she said, "you have begun to read the threads of destiny. You have overstepped your mission, like Phillipidēs did."

He ran at her. He batted back his club. He swung—and struck the scepter. The Oracle pushed him and he vaulted ten feet into the air. He landed harshly, with bone-breaking force. He cried out, having lost his breath. Tears of pain formed in his eyes and the Oracle loomed over him.

Aigon had fled, the coward. He had run away from danger.

The Oracle extended her hand.

Theron grabbed it, allowing her to help him up on his feet.

"You say I read the threads of destiny," he said. "You're a liar."

"You predicted the election of Kunar…"

The thought brought back memories. When he saw the fat, red-face man screaming at the lectern, the thought crossed his mind that he had to be elected—that such a striking figure would not be let to waste.

"You slew my servants," the Oracle said. "You knew when they would strike."

If her words were true, Theron didn't know how or why it happened. All his thoughts, all his assumptions, had been innate and instinctual.

"I alone am allowed to discern the threads of history," said the Oracle. "And yet I will not kill you today, Theron. You have a purpose yet."

Her next words shook Theron to his core.

"Mount Kronos has erupted," she said.

That could only mean one thing: that out of the ashes, the Lord of Chaos had risen again.

DELICA, KERSICA

The gates burst open and Khloë again led the charge. Within hours, the city had been seized, the third as in many weeks.

The sounds of chains breaking lit up the night. Thousands of Elehoi walked free, tasting liberty for the first time.

The Free and Democratic Armies were succeeding. The Kersican League, at war with itself, was failing.

"Mount Kronos has erupted!" one of Khloë's Strategoi told her, and she took it as a sign from heaven that their victory was assured, that their cause was just. How else could she read such an omen?

THE KING

"Agathion the tinkerer," he mused. "Agathion the rich man."

Agathion watched and waited for the lightning to strike. The storm had formed overhead.

He had put together an automaton of brass and bronze. Each plate, each gear, had been forged with excruciating care.

"The King" rotated on a bronze sphere. It was a man made of metal, of shimmering brass. On the automaton's head, Agathion had placed a gold crown embedded with jewels. In the automaton's wiry hand there was a scepter forged of iron.

Agathion leapt back as the lightning struck, filling his laboratory with sparks. The King began to roll this way and that on its metal sphere.

Like he hoped the music box began to strain out its song, and the King raised and lowered his scepter this way and that.

How much could Agathion profit from this? There was no limit. There was no amount of money he couldn't ask for.

KERSEPOLI

Gaia was a different person when the carriage passed through the gates.

Her old strength had returned, her old love for life, her old health. She had slept well, for some reason, ever since she heard Mount Kronos erupted. Had the fires banished all traces of the demiurge?

The more likely solution was that this had all been an illusion, a product of some ailment.

Somewhere on the Sun King's Road, between Kersica and Korthica, Gaia had discarded Nix's charm. She no longer lived in dread. Her body had overcome whatever illness had inflicted it. No more did she have to endure these delusions. She could focus, clearly and with determination, on the task ahead of her, on the promotion of the Kersican League, and of the duties of the nation.

~

The towering white walls of Kersepoli were its most impressive feature; once inside, the buildings were plain, mostly flat-roofed. The most exceptional detail of Kersepoli was its incredible cleanliness. No garbage could be found on its paved streets. The white pavestones gleamed in the sun, and in spaces where homes did not crowd out the sun, there were quiet gardens of palm trees and hyacinths, desert scrubs and queens-of-the-evening. Few Kersican men walked the streets, since war was their life: women and Elehoi, and relatively few of them, went about their business, together with children. It was a different world from Korthos; and yet one which circumstances had wedded them together.

Up above, on the High City, the temple to Tyros lord of

war offered a small contrast to the lack of ornamentation: its towering white pillars of marble gleamed in the sun, as majestic as any other temple in Korthos. But that was not Gaia's destination; instead, it was the palace below.

King Helion and King Straton were in the throne room, seated—in a rarity—together. Usually one was gone, on the field of battle during their continuous wars. Now they remained on their thrones of plain stone. And they were not alone.

A woman was there, garbed in black. Her head was covered in a triangular headdress. Her hands, which she waved as she spoke, were old and wrinkled. Gaia felt like she had met this woman before. Had she seen her in Korthos? Or was she just imagining it?

Soon after Gaia entered, the two kings and the women turned to face her.

King Straton did not recognize Gaia, and King Helion barely registered it seemed—but the woman in black regarded her like an old friend.

Who was she, Gaia wondered. *I should know.* But this woman's name escaped her. She did not look Eloesian.

"Gaia." King Helion remained seated on his throne. "This is Bat Zor, ambassador of Tharta."

She did not look like an ambassador. She had a southron appearance to her. Her eyes were deep and dark, and Gaia wanted to look away, but felt she couldn't.

"Bat Zor," King Helion continued, "Gaia is from Korthos. She was sent to make peace with the Kersican League."

King Helion and King Straton thought they spoke for the entire League. That was the arrogance of Kersepoli, the arrogance of that city. Why remain in a League when Korthos had no voice? Why remain when there was no seat at the table?

"You come to negotiate prices." King Helion smiled. "Tharta has offered to join in partnership with the League. Thénai's doom is sure... will you complain now? Will you exit the League now that victory is assured?"

Gaia had come with demands, but all authority was vested in her.

At the edge of the sword, King Helion had forced crippling prices on Korthian farmers. His henchmen had behaved like robbers to a supposed ally.

It was up to Gaia to make the choice. Korthos had given the authority to her, to make all decisions necessary. On her journey she had passed by those workmen in the wheat fields and the cattle herders in their pastures.

"Total victory," Gaia repeated, murmuring. She did not trust this Bat Zor. Her name declared her a southron. Tharta had decided to yoke itself to the despots of Fharas. Would such an alliance be of interest to the Korthian people, who still remembered the devastation of the Southron War? Could they justify such an alliance with their enemy—even with Tharta, who didn't lift a finger to save Eloesus?

King Helion was there, and King Straton was there, the haughty look in their eyes saying it all: *We are the backbone of the Kersican League, and you can't say no to us.* Perhaps, their arrogance was warranted. In a war against Kersepoli, the Korthicans would surely falter; her people's power lay in its wealth and ingenuity, and—if it came to open conflict—their army would fail before the Kersicans.

And yet Gaia's mind was already made up. She would not settle for anything less than the best for the city she loved, and its people. "It seems you have an ally in Tharta," Gaia said. "You can manage without us. Our farmers are suffering. Your prices are causing poverty and starvation. We will forge our own way. We are resigning from the Kersican League. We want all your troops out of our territory. Every one of them."

King Helion and King Straton remained silent. Bat Zor gazed at her, examining her like a tea leaf. Gaia stormed off, feeling she had failed in her mission. But she had made a decision: she had lifted the heavy yoke of the farmers. She had broken their chains.

~

She left, escorted by hoplites, on her carriage. Compared to the plain buildings of Kersepoli, her gold-embossed wheels and white canvas cover made her seem royal. She pitied these women, garbed in dull robes, who stayed alone in the city while their husband fought in Kersica's endless wars. It had been this way from the beginning: young boys left their mother's side, never to see them again, to train in camps for battle. But Gaia pitied these mothers more than anyone: having their precious children taken from them as a possession of the State. That was unimaginable cruelty.

Their warriors were the best in the world; living every day for the purpose of battle. But at what human cost? Her eyes welled with tears as she passed through the gate, seeing a woman with a toddler. How many months before he was taken from his mother's side?

Life was cruel; the world was a cold and loveless place. Gaia was so lucky to live in Korthos.

MOUNT HYLEA, THEMURIA

Theron had ascended the mountain with Aigon.

He descended it alone, no longer fearing the long reach of the Oracle.

"You have a purpose yet," she had told him amid the sizzling lightning and booming thunder.

Kronos had again manifested. His incarnation now walked the earth. But how and why? Theron didn't know.

~

After an arduous descent, in the cool morning, he passed by the quiet village of Arkadion and embarked down the High Road. The road was now lined with Oraclean columns, carved in the shape of Maids of Prophecy. The Oracle's power was extending over Themuria. Far from being just a religious leader, she had become a power unto her own, one which held almost total control of Arkadion despite its allegiance to Thénai.

And it was growing every day, judging by what these columns and colonnades evinced.

Theron's hatred had not died. His blood still boiled whenever a Maid of Prophecy passed him on the road. But he had a greater purpose now, one which dominated his mind.

~

As the days wore on, and the cool of the mountains began to diminish, so too did the influence of the Oracle. Her power did not yet extend beyond Themuria.

He passed Argon's Table and the City of Nautilos. The world of pines and lakes left him, and he found himself among the hills, in the hot Eloesian sun.

This is what he had known.

And things had changed.

The hills were silent. There was no wind. No shepherds guided their flocks; no cattle herders drove their cows along in search of pastures. It was like the calm before the great sea-storm of Theron's youth—a period of absolute stillness before the waves crashed onto the shore, and ships in the harbor were rent into debris. That night had cost the city untold trouble.

Now, in the total silence and stillness, Theron was certain another storm was coming, a storm of something besides wind and water.

He thought of all the times he's been on this road. He thought of Argon's Table, of the City of Nautilos. He said a prayer for Zoë and Phaido. "Accept them, Amara, into the Fields of Paradise." He would never forget them.

~

Late that day, in the blazing sun, when it seemed every last drop of water on earth would expire into the sky, Theron stopped to rest by a bean sprout. He untied his sandals and ate the raw beans, one after the other. Some said each bean was a soul, sprouting up from the underworld.

Perhaps that is why they tasted so good.

The night set in and the heat drained away. The silence began to break; a wind was blowing from the east. A drizzle began. There was lightning in the distance. And Theron had no shelter.

He braved the rain in his buckskin blanket. The world seemed to quake; the lightning shook and sizzled throughout the earth. The wind blew and a shadow appeared, a shadow Theron recognized: Aigon, centaur, the tutor of heroes.

The Oracle had scared him away. Aigon had abandoned Theron. And yet he showed his face.

Theron stepped out of the buckskin blanket, wearing only his loins.

Aigon was trotting up to him.

"Theron," he said, "my pupil."

He drew closer amid the pouring rain.

He was frowning. Hesitant. Clearly realizing that Theron did not want to see him.

"I'm sorry," he said.

Theron was not one to forgive such slights. "You abandoned me," he replied. "You left me to die."

"And yet you're alive," Aigon said. "Did you slay her?"

Theron didn't want to admit that he had received her mercy—that he had accepted her mercy. He didn't want to say he'd been given a task, and that he'd accepted it. "Kronos is reborn," he announced. "I don't know why or how. I thought I slew him."

"A being of Kronos' power can never be truly slain," Aigon said, "only purged, for a time, from this earth. He is not of this world. He does not belong to the mortal realm, so mortals cannot slay him."

"You are not a mortal," Theron said. "Can you kill him?"

Lightning crackled and thunder rolled. Aigon was smiling. He was sopping wet. "Centaurs are mortals," he said. "We just live longer than you. And when we die, we are dust. We will never ascend to the Fields of Paradise."

Theron wasn't so sure. The goddess Amara wouldn't be so cruel. At least she would allow Aigon, in death, to float in the River of Souls. If Aigon had a soul, like humans, he should not be allowed to perish completely. "What happen to your brothers?" Theron said. "The other centaurs?"

As Aigon began setting up their tent, he started to explain.

"Those days were good," he murmured wistfully as the rain sheeted down and the wind tossed back and forth. "Those days were happier. There was less conflict, less strife…"

"The Archaic World?" Theron asked.

"That is what you call it now," Aigon said as he began hammering in the tent pegs. "It was a golden era. I can only see that now, living in this present age."

"What about the Megarine War?" Theron said. "That surely counts as strife…"

"The Megarine War was a noble war," Aigon said. "It was a war where heroes showed their mettle… where Phillipidēs became a legend. Now your wars are based on selfishness, on borders, on wealth, on power."

"I think your nostalgia is clouding your judgment." Theron wasn't lifting a finger to help Aigon with the tent. "With something so long ago, our memory fails us…"

Aigon remained silent at the argument. Bit by bit, the tent was reaching its final form.

"What happened to the centaurs?" Theron asked. "And why are you still alive?"

"I'm alive because I was different from all my brothers," Aigon said. "My brothers were drunkards, as wild as the satyrs— perhaps a lot wilder. They lost sight of things. But I studied books. I became knowledgeable. I became a tutor to the Kings of Tharta. I became a scholar. Eventually I taught a prince named Phillipidēs."

In plays and stories, centaurs were depicted as wild partiers, ruining the wedding of Old King Ygmalion or overturning the winepresses of Farmer Mageios. But one centaur became wiser than any human, more learned than anyone in Archaic Eloesus—and he stood before Theron now.

"And why are you different?" Theron said. "What's strange about you, Aigon? Why didn't you spend your years drinking wine and feasting?"

Aigon looked at Theron blankly. Clearly, even he did not know the reason. "I haven't drunk a drop of wine in three-hundred years," he murmured, "and I read every book in the Library of Stygidos."

"You didn't answer the question… why?"

Aigon pounded the last tent peg into the earth. Soon the structure held erect, its hide walls blocking out the blowing wind and rain. It was tall enough for a centaur. It was tall enough for Theron. For all the anger he still felt, for all the ill feelings bubbling up after Aigon's cowardice, Theron was glad to see him back.

~

The storm shook the tent; the wind blew and the rain poured, but the squall soon stopped entirely. Theron rested quietly, shutting his eyes and pondering the road ahead. He was sure, even with all his experience, that he did not know its snares and dangers. Kronos had risen again. His power would be unfathomable… almost impossible, even for a hero, to overcome.

~

The next day, traversing the hills, many teams of women on horses rode by: Maids of Prophecy in blue gowns and hoods, bearing daggers. The Oracle was sending them by decree to the site of the catastrophe. Wherever Kronos had materialized, wherever a mortal shell had substantiated, there the Maids of Prophecy would go. They would go, by consent of the Oracle, to the scene of the disaster. They would try their best to contain him, but their powers were limited… as was Theron's. Theron was a hero according to Aigon, with a tutor; but all heroes fell. Heroes were mortals. Eventually, all of them died.

As dusk began to settle in, a great column of smoke appeared in the horizon, an inky black mound rising over the earth. The smell of burning grass and the sight of wildfires weren't an entirely rare sight, especially in the summer, but the circumstances made this ominous. Theron turned off the road and Aigon followed.

A fire was growing, and it was spreading, eating away the dried-up grass. Maids of Prophecy had formed a line around it. They were trying to prevent its spread by throwing wet sacks on the edge and tossing pails of water on the fire.

But why were the Maids of Prophecy so intent on stopping a wildfire? It struck Theron as odd, to say the least.

As the night darkened, the color of the fire became more evident: the flame had a pale look; it was almost green.

It was spreading, as wildfires are wont to do, in a ring. But bit by bit the Maids of Prophecy were managing to extinguish the fire. This fire was different in character, but the water seemed to squelch it.

Theron was now convinced: Kronos was here. Perhaps not close. Perhaps many miles away. But this fire was his creation; this spectral flame, which glowed in strange colors as it died to embers, was his creation. This fire which had turned countless acres to smoldering ash was caused by the Lord of Chaos himself. And the

Lord of Chaos was on the move.

The Maids of Prophecy did not strike at Theron as he brushed by; they didn't try to end his like, they would have just days ago. Theron headed onward, crushing the burnt grass underneath his sandals. Aigon followed behind, hopping over the embers after a moment's hesitation.

"You were too afraid of the Oracle," Theron said. "You abandoned me then… but the Lord of Chaos won't frighten you?"

Aigon laughed. "The Oracle is cruel. She likes to torment… Perhaps it's Kronos' brutality that soothes my fear."

~

The next day, Theron and Aigon located what they believed was the source of the flame: in the ash, an imprint of a foot, resembling a duck's or a lizard's. The footprints continued in a straight path, heading northwest.

Kronos, or his avatar, was heading toward Thénai, the city which he hated above all others.

Aigon took the lead, following the tracks. Soon Theron would meet Kronos, and find victory, or total defeat.

SCYTHION, KERSICA

The Free and Democratic Armies surrounded Scythion's yellow walls, not to pillage, not to plunder or rape, but to bring liberty.

Three thousand Elehoi had been freed in their campaign; three thousand chains, bursting in two, had fallen to the earth. By any means, their mission had been a success. Five cities had been liberated and Scythion would be their sixth.

Morale among Khloë's troops was brimming as it never had before. And final victory was in sight. They grew closer to the Kersican heartland, to Kersepoli itself.

Horns blared; confusion overtook the ranks.

An army was barreling towards them, an army of red-garbed hoplites so large their footsteps sounded like an earthquake.

They broke the ranks of the Thenoans and Khloë was forced into a wild retreat.

~

As the Free and Democratic Armies dispersed, Khloë found herself running alone, her heart weighed by the guilt of her incredible failure. Her warriors had broken their faith and retreated against their instructions; but in war every failure was due to the Strategoi. To the commanders. To *her*.

She had lost track of her horse. In the panic, in the darkness of the night, she had been swept away in the wave of Thenoan hoplites fleeing. She'd lost track of her possessions, even as the shame of their cowardice built.

In Kersica, she knew, any hoplite who fled from battle was executed publicly in the city square. The Free and Democratic Armies had no such method to ensure their troops' bravery. In a moment, when the Kersicans set upon them like a horde, the Free and Democratic soldiers broke into every direction. Panic was allowed to rule the day. Their defeat had been sudden. It had been resounding.

~

When she reached the river, late the next day, she questioned whether she should return home at all. After all, this disaster, this failure, this catastrophe, was all on her shoulders. It was her fault.

Some of her hoplites were swimming across the river as she stood there, while another floated on a makeshift raft. They were scrambling for home.

Was it time for Khloë to accept her true origin, her true race? Was it time to admit she was an amazon first and foremost, and not a human? If she returned to Tigris, she would not have to face her failure.

But facing one's failure was the mark of a warrior. In Amazonia, unless the queen granted mercy, Khloë would meet the executioner. In Thénai, Khloë wasn't sure.

I will face what's coming to me, Khloë told herself. *I will face my failure.*

And so she joined the hoplites, swimming through the murky brown waters of the river. She set foot on Thenoan ground. She had come home, but she had come home in disgrace.

~

She uttered prayers to every god who would listen. She invoked their name, begging them to overlook her cowardice. She walked alone, under the moonlight, as owls hooted and cicadas sang, as the heat of the summer day evaporated and the earth was lit by the mantle of the stars. In time she found herself on the Golden Road, which she had followed on her failed mission of liberation.

You have not failed, she told herself. How many Elehoi had been freed? How many chains had been broken, shattered in two? To the ones they saved from slavery, their mission had been no failure at all. She remembered the looks on their faces, the fear, the uncertainty that came with freedom. Some fled back into the arms of the captors, but most—seeing an opportunity—had fled for Thénai, and freedom. By the law of the Free and Democratic charter, every Elehoi whose chains were broken could become a Thenoan citizen, a full participant in the civic life of the League. She treasured those memories, and kept them alive, as she headed home to face whatever consequences awaited her. She would accept the full force of the law. She would not back away from it.

Days later, Khloë walked through the Lion's Gate.

She realized, among its white-paved streets and red-tile roofs, that Thénai, and not Amazonia, was her home.

SUN KING'S ROAD, KORTHICA

The carriage ride would end soon.

Gaia's dread of the night had been replaced with a greater worry, a worry that reached far beyond her own selfish cares and concerns. The survival of Korthos was at stake; and she had made a judgment, one that she still held firm was right. They had exited the Korthican League, by Gaia's authority. Now that layer of protection was gone—a payment for their dignity and self-rule.

Up ahead, a billow of smoke caught Gaia's eye.

A farmhouse was engulfed in flames. Beyond the wheat fields, in a pasture, cows and oxen lay dead, butchered by swords.

Kersican soldiers were wandering through the fields, swords dripping red with blood.

The Kersicans had declared war on Korthos.

Perhaps Gaia should have expected this. But she didn't. She wept, knowing she was at least partially responsible for this. She bore some of the blame.

No, she thought, as she watched a Kersican murder one of the farmhands, *I bear all the blame.*

~

As the Sun King's Road drew near Korthos, the wheat fields and olive groves began to taper away. The road became crowded with tombstones, of people hoping to gain immortality from these timeless monoliths. Even according to the priests, only heroes and demigods ever reached the Fields of Paradise. So this, a name carved in stone, a mausoleum which told a story, ensured eternal life to those without god's blood in them. Gaia had not stowed away her savings for that. A pauper's grave was all she needed: a shovel, a wooden marker, and six feet of earth.

The Gate of Storms was open, and Kersicans stood guard. The city had surrendered. All Gaia's work had been for naught.

~

She argued furiously with Phaistion in the House of Assembly. With the demiarchs watching, she shouted and screamed, shaking her fist: "I break us free of the Kersican League, and you surrender instantly! I break the chains of the farmers, and you give the Kersicans total control!"

Phaistion, to his credit, remained calm. "The Thartans have joined the League. Our victory is at hand... victory that Korthos will also reap the fruits of."

Gaia wanted to strike Phaistion, right then and there, for giving her the authority to make decisions and then balking at the first sign of trouble. "I served this city honorably for decades... and this is how I'm treated." She was beside herself.

There were a few traces of laughter from the demiarchs in their benches.

"Yes, yes, Gaia," Phaistion said. "You indeed have served Korthos. With honor. With distinction."

The humored looks on the demiarchs said it all. She was a joke to them. Her entire career was laughable.

Gaia stormed out, blood boiling, fingers twitching.

She had poured her life into this city, into its people, into its institutions. Now the falling out with Rogon, the failures to achieve her goals, the decisions which the demiarchs didn't favor, all of that was causing them to abandon her, to laugh at her.

Beyond the Long Walls, past a lengthy road, the harbor city of Alesis opened up to Gaia. Alesis, once isolated, unprotected from its mother city, was now joined to Korthos inexorably.

Gaia had denied it the whole way, but she knew why she was here.

"A ship to Thénai!" cried a sailor. "Last call for passengers…"

She left with the ship at dusk. Gulls swarmed the harbor as they disembarked, as a fair and propitious wind blew them along, swiftly, through the water.

As she stood on the deck, amid the gleaming stars and the full white moon, she realized she had come full circle. Once she had cursed the name of Thénai; now she sought to warn her and her people. Doom was coming to them, certain doom, unless they acted swiftly.

HILL COUNTRY, THÉNAI

The charred grass faded away, and—though Theron could no longer see the webbed, lizard-like tracks—Aigon continued to follow his quarry. Somehow, he was able to follow the trail, even without the obvious markers. To Aigon's keen eyes, each misplaced blade of grass was a clue.

And so the journey continued, even as Theron began to have doubts. Could he overcome Kronos, truly? Could even Phillipidēs, legendary hero, defeat a being so powerful? Uncharacteristic worry was beginning to worm its way through Theron's stomach.

But up on Mount Hylea, amid the raging storm, the Oracle had told him, "You were made for this moment."

Could Theron deny destiny?

~

When, at last, many days of travel later, the gold-colored walls of Thénai appeared in the distance, Aigon took a turn. It appeared that Kronos had taken a different route. He loathed the city of Thénai, but it was not his destination.

"Where is he going?" Theron muttered.

"Toward Stygia," Aigon answered.

Would this long journey end where it had begun, in Lake Stygia in the shadow of Mount Tharnos? It seemed that way.

The tan-colored road leading to Thénai was packed with people. Hoplites were pouring in through the gate, carrying their helmets and swords. Theron wondered what happened... what disaster had befallen them. They were filtering into the city, a dozen at a time. Had the Thenoan army suffered some grave defeat? It seemed that way.

From Thénai, the road to Stygia was a short one, a matter of a few miles. They would reach the submerged ruins before the sun set… and the further along Aigon followed the tracks, the more it became clear that Stygia was exactly where Kronos was headed.

The sun was blazing down on them, and the air wavered in the heat. Amid the wilted cypresses and oak trees, starved for rain, a dark figure scurried into the distance.

"Kronos!" Theron shouted before he'd seen the creature fully.

But it was not Kronos.

The creature running away was hunchbacked.

It was a human, a man, with wild red hair and a beard that almost touched the ground. This was Kunar, having escaped justice. He had usurped the government of Thénai to become king.

He had destroyed the holy temple of Amara and set up the bear-headed abomination of Tyros in its place. He had done such grave damage, and he had gotten away with all of it.

Theron pitched back his club and took off at a sprint.

"Wait!" Aigon shouted.

Theron grabbed Kunar by the scruff of his torn, dirtied tunic. He flailed, suspended in midair.

Kunar's beady eyes were looking at Aigon, then darting back to Theron in a panic. It seemed they had met before.

He had once been Aigon's quarry. And Aigon had let him slip away.

"He's not worth our time," Aigon said. "We have a greater task ahead of us."

Theron wasn't so forgiving. True, the creature squirming from his hand was pitiful, a wretch by any stretch of the imagination. He stunk of many weeks in the wild. Kunar, once the "king" of Thénai, had lived a life of luxury; now, fearing a return to Isteros, he lived like a wild animal in the forest.

"He defiled the Temple of Amara," Theron said. "He destroyed the sanctuary and put another god in her place."

Indeed, what "King" Kunar had done in desecrating Amara's sanctuary was worthy of death in itself. Even compared to the crime of subverting Thénai and destroying its government, the desecration of the temple had no parallel in history.

Kunar was filthy from head to toe, and flies were buzzing around him. The stench emanating from him in the midday heat was making Theron dizzy. He dropped Kunar to the ground. He pitched back *Titan's Fist,* intending to crush his skull. And yet he hesitated.

Kunar was cowering, shielding himself with his hands.

For betraying Thénai, for usurping power, for destroying the government, Theron could let Kunar go. But for defiling Amara's temple, Theron would have revenge. *"I will avenge you, mother,"* he murmured.

In one blow, he crushed Kunar's head. Kunar crumpled up and sank into a ball. A pool of blood grew in size where he lay.

"Was that really necessary?" Aigon said.

Aigon didn't understand. He had lived all this time, secluded, in the mountains. He had lost touch with the gods. He did not know the extent of Thénai's worship for Amara… of their adoration of their mother.

He did not understand the blasphemy of the bear-headed creature which now stood, propped up, in the temple grounds, how deeply insulting it was to the faithful… and how deeply insulting it was to Amara herself. The goddess, the virgin queen of war, had been physically removed from her temple… her image melted into gold ingots, her priestesses replaced with bearded, uncouth priests, her name intentionally scrubbed from the city she loved.

Was it any wonder that disaster had befallen Thénai now?

Aigon brushed Theron's shoulder. "Let's go," he said, regarding the dying Kunar with a genuine sadness in his eyes.

Had Theron gone too far? Of course not. He had no regrets.

~

The dry lake bed of Stygia opened up before them, and in the distance, they saw their quarry.

Pacing back and forth along what once had been a shore, the figure of Kronos seemed to radiate life.

A lizard-like tail protruded from plates of black armor. His left hand was wrapped in a gauntlet far too big for him.

His head was masked in a helmet which Theron recognized instantly: the helmet of his old foe, Rogon.

Like a bug he looked, in the waning sunlight, with antennae-like horns emerging from the helmet.

Kronos cried out in frustration, and his cry echoed through the hills and the mountains. At last he ripped the helmet free, tearing it in two, laying bare his face. What remained of Rogon had mostly left: two horns protruded from his forehead, and scales had begun to form over his skin.

Rogon was changing. Part of him was still there, but most of him was gone. He was transforming into the enemy of Old Eloesus, the Lord of Chaos, who destroyed kingdoms, who unseated kings, who brought terror and instability to the world. His hand was in the destruction of the Archaic World. Now he would return… by Rogon's help.

But how had this happened? How had Rogon, the Dark Captain, been chosen as Kronos' instrument? What circumstances had led him to this point? What had gotten him here?

Kronos—or Rogon—stooped over. His cries, echoing through the hills, had caused a colony of bats to flutter away into the sunlight.

Kronos was keeled over, vomiting. His pain was clear, even from this far away. His shoulders were bulging. He cried out again, louder than before, so loud the trees around him quivered and animals—once secure in the nest—turned and fled.

Wings burst forth from Kronos' back, spitting blood and flesh.

Rogon was not yet Kronos. But he was getting there.

THE MIDDLE SEA

As the ship passed near Salitis, Gaia looked wistfully on, wondering how Hora and Malechon fared now that she was gone. Had Hora's steadfast, abiding faith carried her to better days? Or was Nix a cruel mistress, capriciously tossing her devotees aside?

She pitied Hora for having to live with Malechon. She had married the ghoul for his wealth. There was some love and tenderness between them, but Malechon was strange, and he was private.

She wanted to speak a hymn on her behalf, but Gaia knew the mere words wouldn't help anything... they would just fade away, dissipating into the wind.

~

In the calmer waters of the Thenoan Inlet, *Amara's Grace* continued to benefit from the wind.

This, Gaia thought, *may be the swiftest journey I've ever taken.* The winds had been fortuitous from Korthos to Thénai. Normally a journey like this took a fortnight; now on its sixth day, they were on the home stretch. They were almost to their destination.

These Thenoans, these idealistic Free and Democratic citizens, had no idea what was coming. The combined forces of Korthos, Kersepoli and Tharta had their focus set squarely at Thénai, the one city who dared remain firm, the one city who dared to defy the Kersicans and its military.

Gaia hoped and prayed she would make it to Thenai so that proper preparations could be made. Despite herself, she uttered the words to Nix, "Mother, speed my way..." But the words were just words, vanishing into the wind.

Nevertheless, it was day nine when the harbor of Thénai appeared, together with its walls and fortifications. Innumerable ships lay idle in the docks. For all the wars and conflict abroad, Thénai remained a hive of commerce, and as *Amara's Grace* pulled into the still waters, sailors and local civilians were smiling and laughing amongst themselves. For a doomed city, Gaia thought, the mood was incredibly bright.

On the road, flanked by the Long Walls, white pavestones gleamed in the sun. At even intervals, bronze statues of hoplites guarded the way. Every inch of the road was swept clean and the walls were finished with gold trim. Korthos, in severe debt and financial stress, had spent every spare bit of money in the war effort, enriching the Kersican League treasury. Thénai, however, had spent all its money on its people. Their military had always been far superior to the Kersicans… yet they had held them off completely, at least until now.

Gaia had not brought her servants with her on this mission of betrayal.

In a way it was strange, walking these streets without their support or help. She had not told them where she was going, or why she had come here. Korë was probably worried sick.

In the shadow of Thénai's High City, where the Temple of Amara had stood since time immemorial, the city square stretched like a mosaic of bright reds, greens, and whites. The sound of drums and pipes filled the air, rising above the shouting voices of vendors and merchants who had set up their stalls.

Thénai did not have the military of the Kersican League… but they did have life. Was it enough?

The House of Assembly in Thénai put the House in Korthos to shame. Its marble columns were bright white and trimmed in leaf motifs with gold. On its pediment the words LIBERTY FOR ALL were carved. Its tile shingles gleamed in the sun.

On the marble staircase leading up the building itself, twin bronze statues had been forged: one of Ansolon, founder of democracy; and the other, one whom Gaia recognized instantly, Theron.

Theron, hero of the Southron War, was a man Gaia had met before. She had not treated him kindly, to say the least. But there was something great and wondrous about him, and she remembered him to this day.

The Assembly was in session.

"All four-hundred seats are filled," set the House Guard. "We can't have just anyone poking their noses in."

Gaia had not come all this way just to face failure. "I am an emissary of Korthos," she said, "and I come to tell you an army is gathering against you."

Why had she done this? Why had she defected to their side? There were many reasons, she supposed. The disrespect. The carelessness. The fecklessness.

Was Theron a reason? She did not know, but the bronze image outside had stricken her deeply.

The doors swung open, and the demiarchs sitting on the benches—once shouting over each other—became deathly quiet.

The archon sat on his chair, and by his side was an amazon. Gaia recognized her. This was Khloë.

~

"In short," Gaia said, summarizing everything, "all the forces of Eloesus have been summoned to destroy you. You had best prepare… as best as you can."

She had come as the harbinger of the apocalypse. Now, as much as she did not want to, it was time for her to go home. She was not a Thenoan. She was a Korthian, through and through.

HOUSE OF ASSEMBLY, THÉNAI

The woman from Korthos had entered a room full of squabbling demiarchs, and left one of stunned silence.

Khloë knew full well the peril that had fallen upon them. Already reeling from their defeat, Khloë had only begun to receive punishment. Now, their scattered and demoralized forces would face off against Korthos? Against Kersepoli? Against Tharta?

Every face, sitting on the benches in the House of Assembly, was dour and downcast.

Doom is coming, they knew. *Doom.*

BATTLEMENTS, CITY WALL, THÉNAI

Though the Korthian had warned the Assembly of a great and imminent threat, it was not until weeks later, in the waning days of summer, when the massive army had broken through Bos. From then on, it was mere days until the news, circling like vultures above the dead, built to a fever pitch.

Now Khloë watched with the remnants of the Free and Democratic Army as their enemies emerged, filling the horizon from one edge to the other.

She counted Kersicans and Korthicans, Thartans and Ten Cities men. But there were southrons, here as well.

Amid the marching hoplites and the engines of war, elephants walked toward Thénai like living towers. The King of Kings had joined in the effort, to bring final judgment to the city which had humiliated him.

The horns were blowing and the battle standards waving.

Then, when they had gotten within a few dozen yards, panic set into the ranks. Something was happening. Khloë didn't just know what.

OUTSIDE THÉNAI

Rogon had almost changed fully, for good.

He was within hours of achieving true power, when no mortal could kill him.

Theron lurked just yards away.

Kronos had been attracted to the sight of the army.

In days of old, Kronos had led armies through his deputies. He had turned cities and kingdoms against one another. He had done all these things for the sake of spreading panic and bloodshed, of causing death and destruction. Kronos wanted chaos more than anything… chaos and spiraling devastation.

Somehow, in this army, in his crafty mind, he thought he could engineer chaos once again and bring Eloesus, his old enemy, to its knees.

He had only moments before Rogon completed his transformation completely. When Kronos was embodied, in full, Theron could not kill him.

It was now or never.

~

The armies of Tharta, Kersepoli and Kersica—taking notice of the creature before them—sounded the alarm.

An arrow struck Kronos in the chest, but burned to ash on contact.

Kronos roared, and his roar carried all around, deafening in its tone and volume.

The elephants broke free from their mahouts' control. Stampeding every which way, they sent hoplites, Kersican and Korthian alike, scrambling in each direction in a stampede.

Strategoi called out in loud voices, attempting to regain

control. But they were largely powerless as the elephants trampled over soldiers. One by one the mahouts used their hammers and pegs to end the beasts' lives and stop their reign of terror.

By now the armies were focused not on Thénai, but on Kronos.

A wave of arrows swept toward Kronos, but he raised his hand and all burned into dust. He lurched forward and—seeing the cold green scales, the crimson eyes, the red halo which glowed around his head—the hoplites screamed curses and began to fall back.

Kronos lifted his black steel gauntlet and the swords and spears flew toward him like a magnet, then bent into worthless shapes.

By now full-scale panic had overtaken the army.

They began to break rank and fall apart.

Theron lifted *Titan's Fist* and gave his beloved weapon a kiss. It was now or never. Rogon had almost completed his apotheosis.

Theron charged across the field, screaming. Kronos had hardly turned around when Theron's club shattered his skull.

As Kronos slumped to the ground, he began to revert to human shape once more. The scales began to fade. His crimson eyes ceased their glow.

And Theron collapsed in utter exhaustion.

HIGH CITY, THÉNAI

The war would continue, Khloë knew.

But for now, the greatest disaster had been averted.

Theron, having left in a quiet manner, had returned to Thénai as a lion; he had slain every one of Tyros' priests, hanging them on trees in the High City.

He had ordered the bear-headed statue of Tyros to be melted down into its commensurate parts of silver and gold.

He had defaced every shrine. He had burned the wooden images. He had hauled out every relic for destruction and then cleansed the temple ceremonially with incense.

Now he stood by in his lion's skin, waiting as the statue of Amara was returned to its place.

A year had passed since the armies had been driven away… in a miracle, by a man many considered a demigod but who all considered a hero: Theron.

For a year, goldsmiths and metallurgists under the supervision of the inventor Agathion had labored on an image fit for Amara. Her skin was of ivory, her eyes of sapphires, her lips of ruby and carnelian, and her breastplate and spear of purest gold. She stood thirty feet tall, just barely fitting underneath the temple's immense roof.

It was a new day in Thénai. A new day, a hard day in some ways… but a new one.

~

That night, with Amara's temple rededicated, and her priesthood restored, Khloë led Theron out of the city gates, into the fields. For months he had not seemed himself. He did not seem happy.

"Theron," Khloë whispered, her hands on his shoulders. "What's wrong with you?"

Amid the green grass and blue skies, a rock warbler was singing her song. The sounds of the city had faded away, and a wind was blowing, rushing through the trees.

Theron, as always, wore sandals. Flies were buzzing around his lion's skin. He was not comfortable in the city—that much was clear. But something larger than that was eating at Theron, Khloë's friend.

So she repeated her question. "What's wrong?" she said.

Theron sighed. He looked out into the darkness of the night. Cicadas and frogs were singing. "This life isn't for me," he said.

The centaur who was following Theron had told him as much.

"Aigon said I won't be happy here," he had told Khloë months ago.

Khloë had strenuously objected. Theron had finally done as she'd suggested… return to civic life in the city she called home.

Now, looking at him here in the darkness of the night, wearing sandals, with a club in his hand, she realized she'd made a mistake. She had erred in giving him advice. He was not meant for the bustling streets, for the marketplaces and the arguments of philosophers. There was no place less fitting for him than Thénai, even though he'd once called it home.

"I'm leaving," Theron muttered.

In the darkness, Khloë hadn't noticed the pack Theron was wearing. From the shadows, a donkey clopped toward them, loaded with saddlebags.

"I think you should," Khloë said, "even though I don't want you to. Even though I'm your friend."

"The temple is restored." Theron grabbed the reins of the

donkey. "But there is still a lot of work to be done. A lot of problems to solve."

"And you will solve them." Khloë touched Theron's cheek. He had not shaved in days.

How handsome he was, how dark, how sullen in the moonlight. She grabbed a hold of him and locked him in a deep kiss.

"I've wanted to do that for a long time," she said.

Theron pushed her away. "It was nice knowing you, Khloë. It was nice, fighting alongside you. Being your friend."

The words rang hollow, insincere. Khloë watched as Theron's most legendary hero vanished into the night.

MOUNT THARNOS

"I'm here, like you asked," Theron said to Aigon, who loomed above him on a rocky outcrop.

"Yes, you are," Aigon said. His teeth gleamed in the moonlight. "A hero's life is what a hero needs. There are more Carceran Lions to slay, more Maids of Prophecy to vanquish…"

"Indeed," Theron said. "It's a hero's life for me…"

HOUSE OF THE SATYR, KORTHOS

How quickly the winds of fortune change, how capricious are the gods in their heavenly home.

Workmen were installing tile shipped in from the Blessed Isles. Only the whitest marble would do for Gaia.

She had said good riddance to her husband of many years.

She had received a government post.

Gaia was back on top, and the troubles of the prior years had been all forgotten.

She watched the workmen laying the marble over the mortar, wearing a white silk dress she'd purchased from the market and drinking fine red wine which had been produced in the rich volcanic fields outside Mount Kronos.

"Gaia," she whispered to herself, "you are back on top."

She pranced around her home throughout the day, until well after sundown, when she had a meal of roast quail, seasoned in Fharese spices, and a bowl of steamed legumes better than any southron could make it.

She slept in a bed of Khazidean linens, on pillows stuffed with goosefeathers, in a nightgown of samite threaded with gold silk.

She took a sip of wine before bed. "Here's to me," she whispered, looking into her bedside mirror.

Out of the shadows of her closet stepped the demiurge, his body black, a mantle of the night, his eyes red, as red as blood.

Gaia screamed as she slipped into paralysis.

He is back, she thought. *He is back!*

EPILOGUE: FARSEER

Bat Zor closed her eyes on the balcony of Tharta's royal palace. She breathed deep in the face of the wind. She focused intently.

Her body was old, her soul and mind weary. Her skill at far sight was becoming inaccessible.

Nevertheless she saw Tharta's doom writ in the threads of destiny: utter destruction, not in her lifetime nor in Zubeida's, but in the future.

She uttered prayers to the new gods in holy heaven, and to the old gods who lived on in nightmare. It was not her will. But they had made up their minds.

When Tharta burned, Eloesus would fall with it; and with it, the world.

She turned to toward the sea and saw a shadow rising in the west: a horned beast with iron claws, as tall as a mountain.

The mirage vanished but Bat Zor sank to her knees. She wept and cried, begging the gods to change the fate of this world, to stop the shadow in the west from rising.

CONTINUED IN BOOK 7, 'QUEST FOR A HERO'…

GLOSSARY

CALENDAR

1: Alphaios (March)
2: Pheidos (April)
3: Dektros (May)
4: Soloön (June)
5: Tyron (July)
6: Amaron (August)
7: Ergon (September)
8: Nichion (October)
9: Phimetron (November)
10: Kryon (December)
11: Titanion (January)
12: Etapion (February)

CURRENCY

Thalos: A small silver coin, worth one-fourth a doukos. Plural thalon.

Doukos: The standard silver coin across Eloesus. It takes many forms but generally has the city's patron god cast onto the front and the victory laurel wreath on the back. Plural doukon. One doukos is about the daily wage of a skilled laborer.

Oros: A gold coin, worth fifty doukon. Plural orhon.

Talent: A unit of measurement, worth one-thousand doukon.

TERMS

Alabastros: The king of the gods in the Eloesian pantheon. He is revered especially by the Thartans. As king of the gods, he is considered to preside over kingship, leadership, and royalty. He is often depicted as a wise old man. His favored animal is the lion.

Amara: The goddess of motherly love in the Eloesian pantheon. In Thénai and the Amazonian Isles, she is also the goddess of wisdom and battle. Although a mother, she is a virgin. Eloesian legend states she is the daughter of Alabastros and the Earth. Her brother is Tyros, god of war.

Amazons, the: A race of people living in the coastal islands off the Eloesian shore. Their women are far stronger and—some argue—more intelligent than their men. Though they look similar to humans, amazons and humans cannot breed. The child of an amazon and a human is always stillborn.

Amazonia: A term for amazon lands. Amazonia encompasses the islands of Jogheira, Straiteira, Agathë, Kalormenë and a few smaller islands.

Bactris: A city in Korthica.

Barbarian: A non-Eloesian. The Isteroi and the people of the Ten Cities are often considered barbarians.

Ansolon: The founder of the Thenoan democracy and perhaps all democracies. He led a popular revolt against the tyrant king and seized power over the government.

Archaic World, the: A term generally referring to the time period before the Amazon-Eloesian War, circa 50 years before the consecration of the temple (B.C.T.) or before the Fall of Stygia, ten years later.

Arkadion: A village, the largest in the wilds of Themuria, called the Bride of the Wilderness. It is allied to Kersepoli.

Book of Ceremonies: In Korthos, one of a series of books recording marriages, funerals and namings. Almost every citizen is recorded within, since the Temple of Arephon is the site of all such ceremonies.

Brecko: The god of pleasure, wine and theater, as well as shepherds. His worship is centered in Arkadion in Themuria. He is depicted as a man with goat legs, like a satyr, but without their furry mane or pointed ears. He is considered the father of the satyrs. The panther is considered his sacred animal, though panthers do not live in Themuria. According to legend, Brecko's mother, Amara, was tricked by the goddess Nix into mating with a goat.

Cupids: Creatures inhabiting Themuria in certain times of the year. Though very rarely seen, they are said to possess miniature bows and poison arrows which causes madness and hysteria to those they strike.

Civic gods: The gods considered sacred to a particular city. Tharta favors Alabastros; Korthos, Nix and Arephon; Kersepoli, Tyros lord of war; and Thénai, Amara.

Dys: A land far west from Eloesus across the sea, on the border of the ocean, little known and little explored. Thartan settlers planted cities along its western and southern coasts: Mageios, Lornadion, and Agathion.

Elehoi: A large underclass, forming the majority of the population of Kersica. They are slaves, captives from Kersepoli's numerous wars, and all Eloesian by birth. The name means "little Eloesian" or "Eloesian-like."

Fharas: A vast empire, by far the strongest power in the world. It is ruled by the King of Kings, who is considered a living god. The word Fharas and Fharese also refers to a certain region and people—the heartland where the empire began.

Fields of Paradise: According to Eloesian religion, a region of heaven where the heroes and certain virtuous mortals go after death.

Gate of Storms: The main gate of Korthos. One of the city's most defining monuments, it is dedicated to Arephon, patron god of Korthos, the lord of storms and lightning. From the Gate of

Storms, the Sun King's Road continues to Kersepoli.

Herodium: In Eloesus, a shrine built specifically for heroes as well as semi-divine demigods. The greatest of the herodiums is in Tharta, honoring Phillipidēs.

Hoplite: The traditional soldier in the Eloesian army. Each hoplite has a helmet and a breastplate, a spear and a shortsword, in addition to an iron-rimmed wooden shield. When fighting, he locks shields with his fellow hoplites, forming an impenetrable wall as long as he holds formation.

Ink-of-Tyrhenos: A cosmetic product created from squid's ink, used to darken eyelashes and hair. It is named after Tyrhenos, the legendary king of the cyclops, for reasons unknown.

Isteroi: See Isteros.

Isteros: A region in the north of Eloesus, along the river Ister. The Isteroi speak a dialect of Eloesian but are thought to be outsiders, due to their pallid complexions and frequently red hair. Arctos, the capital, is much smaller in size than other Eloesian cities.

Kersepoli: A large city, one of the four greatest in Eloesus. It is the most militaristic of the Eloesian cities and is ruled by two kings, either of whom may overrule the other.

Kersican League: A union of Eloesian city-states with Kersepoli as the head. Megaris and the Ten Cities announced their membership within months of the Southron War's ending; a small handful of other cities in mainland Eloesus also joined.

Korthos: A large city, one of the four greatest in Eloesus. It is ruled by an Assembly, elected by the people, and an archon, elected by the Assembly.

Lord of Chaos: A term for the demon lord Kronos. Kronos is considered to be a master of strife and discord, delighting in spreading conflict and war.

Megarine War, the: An ancient conflict, shrouded in myth and legend, between the cities of Tharta and Megaris. According to ancient tales, the king of Megaris Sosimon fell in love with Prophylaia, the queen of Tharta. Sosimon abducted Prophylaia and the king of Tharta declared war.

Mirror of Truth: A magic mirror which, according to myth, the goddess Amara gave to the hero Phillipidēs. He used it to kill the Stone Gorgon, whose gaze turned its enemies to rock.

Nix: The goddess of secrets and whispers, her followers call her the Gray Lady or the Queen of Sorcery. She presides over the knowledge of herbs—healing and poisonous—as well as hidden knowledge, wisdom, and the metals iron and silver. She is feared throughout Eloesus, though her name is invoked for protection from the unquiet dead. Korthos was historically the center of her worship. Her favored animals are the owl and the dog. According to Eloesian legend, she is the daughter of Tyros, god of war, and Seladora, goddess of nature. She was hated by her parents and cast out of the household.

Oraclean style: A style of architecture which, until recently, was known only in ruins in Eloesus. Oraclean columns are carved in the shape of Maids of Prophecy. Motifs of eyes and hourglasses are common.

Powder-of-Adamantis: A cosmetic white powder, created in the city of Adamantis. The means of its making are a carefully guarded secret.

Phillipidēs: An Eloesian legendary hero, the son of a Thartan noble who fought in the Megarine War.

Sollust: The god of healing, worshipped primarily in the colonies of Dys. His main temple is in the Dysian city of Mageios, where the ill are offered a combination of medicines and faith healing. His sacred animal is the serpent, and nonvenomous snakes run free in his temple, supposedly offering his healing charms.

She of the Silvered Sword: A phrase referring to Nix, the goddess of secrets. The exact meaning of the phrase is no widely known, but Nix is often depicted as wielding a silver sword.

Stratemon: According to myth, a hero who slew the Queen of Monsters, Myrtolax. Stratemon, the King of Nissos, was supposedly given a sword of fire and a mirror shield by Amara on Mount Hylea.

Stratego: In the Eloesian military, a general or commander.

Stygidos: An ancient city, now ruined, which gave its name to the region of Stygia. In the Archaic World, it was the greatest of the cities in Eloesus, by far wealthier and older than Tharta. Scholars believe it was located somewhere near Thénai.

Ten Cities: A confederation of ten city-states, west from Eloesus across a desert, with Megaris as its head. The Ten Cities take great pride in their half-southron, half-Eloesian identity. They say they form a bridge between Fharese despotism and Eloesian democracy.

Titan: A powerful kind of giant, present only in Themuria but once widespread in Eloesus. They are called the "Sons of Chaos" and are often heralded by thunder and lightning. Meeting one of them is considered a death sentence.

Tigris: The largest city of the Amazons, having about thirty thousand residents plus half as many slaves. It is located on the island of Jogheira. The amazon queen, Daphnë, rules from here.

Tharta: A great city, considered the chief in Eloesus. It is ruled by a king but has certain limited forms of democracy.

Thénai: A large city, one of the four greatest in Eloesus. It is ruled by an Assembly, elected by the people, and an archon, elected by the Assembly.

Thenoan League: A union of Eloesian city-states with members across the Middle Sea. The headquarters of the League is in Thénai, where the League treasury is located and all League decisions are made.

Tyros: The god of war. He is revered in Kersepoli and Isteros; yet he is viewed as never favoring one city over the other, delighting only in battle itself and spilled blood. According to Eloesian legend, he was the son of Alabastros and the Earth. His sister is Amara and his daughter is Nix, whom he hates.

ABOUT THE AUTHOR

Cursed at birth with a wild imagination, Andrew Cooper spent his youth dreaming of worlds more exciting than Earth.

He is a graduate of the Odyssey Writing Workshop. His stories have appeared in Morpheus Tales, Fear and Trembling, Residential Aliens and Mindflights, among others.

CONTACT THE AUTHOR

Visit **www.aj-cooper.com** to sign up for the newsletter and stay up-to-date on new releases.

Find him on Facebook at:

www.facebook.com/AJCooperauthor